THE SPIDER:
THE SPIDER AND THE FACELESS ONE

THE SPIDER AND THE FACELESS ONE

By Grant Stockbridge

POPULAR PUBLICATIONS • 2024

CHAPTER 1
DEATH-TRAP FOR THE SPIDER

THE LOUNGE corridor that led to the terrace garden of the Hesperides Club was deserted. Inside, warm lights cast a subdued glow; the thumping rhythms of a swing band fought against the wolf whine of the November winds. At the end of the corridor, the French doors were tightly sealed. No patron of the club would wish to brave that terrace, open to the arctic breath from the near-by river. Yet now, someone was outside. The knob of the door turned slowly. And against the lighted panes of glass, there was a queerly distorted shadow, as if a man with curiously hunched shoulders crouched there, working on the lock!

Muted shouts and a muffled shot from outside slapped across the musical murmur that sifted into the corridor from the huge dining-room, but these sounds were swallowed in the universal thump of the orchestra. There was a brittle snap of breaking metal... and the door thrust open! A few hard, fine snowflakes whirled in through the opening and the curtains shivered in the cold. Then a figure whipped into the corridor, the door clapped shut—and a man whirled to send his piercing blue-gray gaze stabbing through the dim reaches of the club.

The shouts outside were louder, but there were no more shots... yet!

The man's lipless mouth twisted in a thinly bitter smile, and

"He's dead," the leader said slowly. "He's got to be dead!"

long silent bounds carried him along the carpeted hallway. A broad-brimmed black hat was drawn low over his brows, and as he ran, a long, black cape whipped and bellied from his shoulders. A handkerchief was bound about his right hand, and the white cloth was stained with sinister red!

A dozen feet ahead, the door of a private dining-room opened quietly, and a waiter stepped into the corridor. His head was bent, and there was a knowing smile on his lips, slyness in his eyes. He straightened and saw the racing figure, and the smile grew lop-sided on his lips; his mouth strained with the beginning of a scream that could not drag itself free of his lips.

"My God! *The Spider!*"

THE SPIDER'S leap was as fierce as the charge of a tiger! His left fist cut a crisp arc to the waiter's chin! He eased the man to the floor and, with a swift glance behind him, sped on! He whipped around the corner toward the great arch that was the main entrance to the dining-room!

An instant later, the terrace doors burst open and four men spilled into the corridor. They were hatless, without overcoats, faces burnished by the wind. Guns were in their fists and their eyes were hot and eager. Their leader pointed a hand toward the prostrate waiter, and the hand trembled.

"He came this way!" the man said, and there was a tremor in his voice, too, like the whine of a dog when the scent is hot. "Rex, stay here! Watch those doors! Mac is bringing the other boys around the front, and I'll get Duncan. By God!" He lifted a clenched fist on which the knuckles shone, white as bone. "By God, *we've got the Spider!*"

Three of his men raced on. The man called Rex stood beside the closed terrace doors. His eyes searched the doorways, the corridor. They even flicked to the ceiling. It was all right for Butch to leave him here to watch for the Spider, but God in heaven, what chance did one man stand against the Spider? That guy just wasn't *human*. Let a guy step outside the law, and try to grab himself a little easy money—and down upon him came the Spider! You could bribe cops and judges; a smart mouthpiece could wriggle you through most any scrape, but from the Spider, there was no chance of protection at all!

Rex clutched his gun until his forearm ached. Behind him, the wind rattled the door… and he jumped two yards away from it, whipped about with a shaking gun-hand.

"Geez!" he whispered. "I wish the gang would come back!"

Just short of the arched entrance to the main dining-room of the Hesperides Club, the gunmen had gathered in a tight knot.

Their wary eyes skimmed over the laughing guests inside the doorway. They were in a side alcove off the main lobby. Telephone booths lined one wall and no one heeded them. The man called Butch stood tautly, with his lips folded in against each other. His breath made rasping sounds in his nostrils.

A compact, broad-shouldered man, smoothly plastered head thrust forward aggressively, swung around the corner and confronted.

"What the hell is this, Butch?"

Butch faced him. His words pushed out like bits of metal between clamping teeth. "The Spider! He came in here! Duncan, we've got him!"

Duncan's cold gambler's eyes narrowed. "By God, if we can get him, I'd almost be willing to wreck the club! You boys spread out. Doors plugged? Good! Mac, stay here. The rest of you… *Come on!*"

The man called Mac had a sly, pointed face. His eyes were wide, round and palely shallow, the eyes of the killer. "The dining-room, Duncan," he said softly, the words almost lisped.

Duncan glanced toward him, took short choppy strides toward the main arch. His brittle glance swept the floor before settling on the headwaiter.

"Any new guests in the last five minutes?" he snapped.

"Nearly ten," the headwaiter murmured. "The Saxon-Thompsons, Miss van Sloan.…"

"To hell with them!" Duncan whirled to the others, gestured with a tautness that made his arm move jerkily. The men wedged behind him. They moved on their toes, eyes darting everywhere, hands thrust into gun pockets. Mac stood against the wall.

Just let the Spider pop out now from somewhere. This superman talk was a lot of rot. There wasn't any man you couldn't kill with a bullet in the right place. He'd put his mark on the Spider!

He grinned… then straightened.

A **WAITER** with a worried frown swung around the corner

from the main entrance. "You Mac?" he grunted. "There's a call for you in Duncan's office. Says come quick!"

Mac said, "Yeah? For me?"

He started toward the waiter, and the man turned away. They were around the corner for perhaps ten seconds, then Mac came bounding back.

"You get the number!" he called after the waiter. "I can't leave!"

His eyes stabbed quickly, hotly about the corridor, centered on the phone booths... on the booth at the very end. His round pale eyes stretched a little wider and the smile on his mouth became a twisted, sly grimace. He touched his tongue to his lips.

"Hey, you!" he snapped at the head-waiter. "Get Duncan, and get him fast!"

The headwaiter stiffened, stepped into the corridor. "Were you talking to me?" he asked indignantly.

Mac's head swung toward him deliberately, and his pale eyes fell on those of the headwaiter. The man quivered. "Yes, sir! Mr. Duncan, I'll get him!"

Mac kept his eyes on the booth, and Duncan came swiftly, slapping his heels down hard into the softness of the cushioned carpet. Mac pointed with his chin, his lips scarcely moving.

"The end booth," he murmured. "See that piece of black stuff sticking out through the door! That's the Spider's cape!"

Duncan drew in a quick, hard breath. His right hand snapped across his chest, came back into sight with a gun from an underarm holster.

"You mugs close up this corridor," he whispered to the men

7

at his back. "We don't want nobody from the dining-room butting in."

Duncan moved forward on his toes. Mac slipped from his side and came at the booth door from the other side. Their eyes shone, and their breath was noisy between colorless lips.

"Burn him down?" Mac formed soundless words.

Duncan nodded curtly. His teeth began to show between his lips. They were flat against the wall, against the other booths on each side of that partly opened door. Duncan reached out his hand, set it on the handle. He drew in a slow breath, his shoulders swelled. Then he whipped open the door!

With a muffled shout, Mac leaped forward, his gun lifted, ready. Duncan's gun was cradled against his hip.

White fumes roiled out of the opened door. Tendrils of smoke curled up toward the ceiling, swarmed about the shaded lights. There was that smoke, and the little tag-end of a black cape… and that was absolutely all. The booth was empty!

Duncan ripped out a harsh oath, spun toward Mac.

A booth five doors up the line was pushed open, and a man stepped out—a tall smiling man with a lithe self-confidence in his every movement, with his head, capped in crisp black hair, held commandingly. His evening dress was tailored perfection.

"What's the trouble, Duncan?" he drawled pleasantly. "Someone attempt to hold you up?"

Duncan whipped toward the man. For an instant, his face was out of control. His mouth was twisted by ugly rage, his eyes glittering. It was only an instant, then his calm gambler's mask dropped into place again, and he was smiling.

"A chiseler did a sneak on us, Mr. Wentworth," said Duncan suavely. "I hope we haven't disturbed you."

Wentworth smiled. The gesture of his right hand, a lean, delicately shaped hand, but powerful, was easy. "Not at all, Duncan," he said easily. "I hope you catch your... chiseler. I dislike such rabble."

"A chiseler did sneak out on us, Mr. Wentworth," said Duncan. "It's been a long time since we've seen you here. Welcome to the Hesperides." He stepped toward Wentworth... *and thrust out his right hand!*

WENTWORTH'S EASY smile did not fade, though he knew well the significance of Duncan's offered handclasp. These killers knew that the Spider had been wounded in the right hand... and here was Wentworth on the spot where the Spider had vanished in a cloud of smoke! The wound, no more than a bullet-burn, but damnably painful nonetheless, was covered now with a swift hemostatic collodion. And Wentworth, calmly, deliberately, accepted Duncan's handclasp. Duncan's fingers clamped down with a vise-like pressure, and his powerful thumb dug into the back of Wentworth's wounded hand!

Pain shot up Wentworth's arm and jarred against his nervous system like a thousand jabbing knives, but it was not for nothing that Wentworth lived his double life; on one hand the wealthy gentleman of leisure, clubman, sportsman; and on the other, that secret avenger of the night, that champion of preyed-upon humanity—known as the Spider! His clasp of Duncan's hand was natural, easy, and the careless smile of his lips never wavered!

Through long seconds, Duncan held that grip... then he

relaxed it and stepped back, and there was puzzlement in his black eyes.

"You give your guests a warm welcome, Duncan," Wentworth said easily. "I'm sorry I haven't dropped by before, but I've been… rather on the run lately!"

Duncan faltered, "I hope we didn't disturb you."

Wentworth waved his right hand carelessly, a lean, powerful hand, but delicately sensitive in shape. "Not at all. I couldn't reach my party, and I didn't like to leave my number. Always unsatisfactory, don't you think?" He turned toward the close-pressed rank that closed the corridor. "I hope you catch your chiseler!"

Unostentatiously, he tucked his right hand into his trouser pocket. The blood was squeezing out through the collodion… and these wolves would need no more than a glimpse of blood upon his right hand to close in with blazing guns! Such was their fear and hatred of the Spider, they would risk anything at all to bring him down!

He moved casually toward the corridor guards. His gray-blue eyes looked beyond them. The head waiter was already bowing obsequiously… And that row of killers, of men panting for the

10

/RICHARD WENTWORTH

life of the Spider, lawless criminals who lived by the gun… These men stepped aside and made a passage for Wentworth without waiting for an order from Duncan! Such was the force of the man, Wentworth.

The headwaiter bowed again, "This way, Mr. Wentworth," he said loudly. "Miss van Sloan is waiting!"

Mac was at Duncan's elbow. "You heard what he said, didn't

you? He tried to get somebody, and wouldn't leave his number. Well, look here. Somebody phoned me in your office, sent word by the waiter. I turned my back for maybe ten seconds...."

"Ten seconds," murmured Duncan. "Time enough. Yes, time enough for him to leave one booth and duck into another... But he didn't flinch when I clamped down on his hand."

"He's got that hand in his pocket now," said Mac....

RICHARD WENTWORTH strolled easily across the dining-room of the Hesperides. A dozen people nodded to him eagerly, or tried to detain him at their tables, but he murmured his excuses and pushed on. He knew that Duncan's eyes were still on him, and that the men would not so soon, or so easily, drop their search for the Spider. He was still in the deathtrap! After all, the Spider had killed one of their number tonight, one of their experts who would be hard to replace—an expert in the cowardly, vicious crime of arson!

Wentworth's eyes met those of Nita van Sloan across the last fifty feet of the dining-room and saw the smile move her full soft lips. His stride lengthened, and there was, perhaps, a pang in his breast; not that he regretted his task, or the duties to which he had pledged himself. But it was hard on Nita always to live thus in peril. A pity, a great pity that they were not what they seemed—two people very much in love and out for an evening's entertainment....

"I hope, my dear," he murmured, "that I haven't kept you waiting long?"

"A year or so," Nita laughed up into his face. "At least five minutes."

Wentworth clasped her hands… with his left, dropped an order for martinis to the attentive waiter as he slid into a chair opposite Nita. She leaned toward him with her handkerchief.

"Dear," she said, "you should be more careful when you keep me waiting! Who was she?" She touched his mouth corner with the handkerchief, dabbing away a bit of the Spider make-up which he had missed. Under her breath, she whispered. "Duncan is coming this way. Four men backing him, separately. Do you need my gun?"

Wentworth sighed, lips smiling though his gray-blue eyes were keen and cold. "I hoped to conceal that blonde from you," he said, and softly, "Knock over your glass and break it!"

Nita leaned back easily, but her hand, returning to her side, jarred her water glass toward the floor. Wentworth grabbed for it as it shattered… and gashed the back of his right hand! With an exclamation of annoyance, he clapped a handkerchief to the wound—and looked up into Duncan's coldly watchful eyes.

"I seem to be hard on your glassware this evening, Duncan," he said easily, and uncovered his hand.

Duncan's solicitous tones held an undercurrent of mockery. "I hope it's not a severe wound, Mr. Wentworth."

Wentworth smiled, "It might have been so much worse. Did you want something?"

Duncan uttered an exclamation. "Stupid of me. That wound quite cut it out of my mind. There's a phone call for you… in a booth in the hall."

"Somehow," Wentworth murmured, "I have an aversion to phone booths tonight. Have a phone plugged in here, Duncan."

He turned back to Nita, who was engaged in binding his cut hand with the napkin. "It's really nothing at all, dear," he said.

Duncan stood an instant longer by the table, then whipped about and went striding choppily across the dining-room.

"He's not satisfied," Nita said quietly. "He'll be back. What do you want me to do?"

"Nothing just now," Wentworth told her. "In a little while, we'll leave. I dropped my cigarette-lighter while paying a call this evening...."

Nita could scarcely control her start. In those few words, she knew the whole story. She knew that Wentworth's cigarette-lighter held a device in its base for imprinting the seal of the Spider, and she knew where that seal was placed—upon the foreheads of those he killed in his coldly just execution of those who were outside the law!

A young couple strolled past, talking excitedly. "Best fire I've seen in years!" the man was exclaiming. "That old tenement burned like paper."

"And good riddance, I say!" the girl cried, and laughed.

Wentworth's lips lost their smile. Thoughtless fools! "Five children died in that fire," he told Nita quietly. "It was a touch-off! Arson!"

Nita's shoulders shuddered a little, and she drew the fur scarf about them. "So that was where you went," she whispered. "That man deserved death!"

Wentworth glanced up as the waiter set the martinis before them with a flourish. Duncan was returning with another waiter who bore a table phone. The smile on his lips was quiet, and Nita did not need to read his thoughts. She knew that the Spider had ferreted out the guilty man—and that he had got his deserts! But the cigarette-lighter, and the bullet burn across the back of his hand... and these cold-jawed men with their terrible, hidden guns....

Wentworth lifted the martini in his left hand, and Nita gaily clinked her glass against his. "Death and destruction..." Wentworth murmured.

"The phone, Mr. Wentworth," Duncan interrupted suavely.

Wentworth laughed, and finished the toast... "to all care and sorrow, my dear!"

DUNCAN GESTURED to the waiter, who plugged in the phone... and Wentworth took it—in his left hand. He was leaving no prints of his right hand here. It had been gripping the cigarette-lighter when a bullet had burned across its back, paralyzing the grip of his fingers. And he needed the gun in his left hand, and needed it badly! There had been no time for anything except flight. He lifted the phone.

"Richard Wentworth here," he said, with a quiet smile at Nita. He had only half-believed in the reality of this phone call, but he knew the voice that cracked secretly in his ear.

"Danger, Major!"

Wentworth's nerves tautened. Only Jackson, who had served under him in the war and was still his top-sergeant, called him 'Major.' And Jackson was at police headquarters on the Spider's special business. But while Wentworth's nerves keyed to the excitement in Jackson's voice, even Nita could see no change in his smile.

"Yes," he said.

Jackson already was rushing on. "Police headquarters is turned inside out. Anonymous tip where a body can be found with Spider seal on forehead—and beside the body, a cigarette-lighter *with the Spider's fingerprints on it!*"

Wentworth frowned slightly. "He must have been in a hurry to have been so careless," he said, already preparing for an abrupt departure. "The matter is getting expert attention, I take it?"

"Headquarters blew up!" Jackson chuckled. "Kirkpatrick left with motorcycle escort ninety seconds ago!"

"In that case," Wentworth said quietly, "we'll hurry right along, of course. Certainly, you may use the other car. And I suggest you hurry. Lucky you knew where to reach me."

Those last few words had told the quick-witted Jackson what to do—get another car and speed to the Hesperides Club. Frowning deeply, Wentworth handed the phone to the waiter. Under the watchful eyes of Duncan, he sat thoughtfully for a moment, then lifted his eyes gravely to Nita.

"There's hardly any way to break bad news, my dear," he said quietly. "Your cousin, Gregory, just had the misfortune to be hit by an automobile."

"Gregory!" Nita burst out, rising at once to her feet. "Is he hurt badly?"

Wentworth shook his head. "Can't tell yet. Fortunately, he was struck near my apartment, and the doorman recognized him, had him carried right in."

Duncan slid Nita's chair aside. His eyes were puzzled. "I hope,

Miss van Sloan, you will find this less serious than you anticipate."

Wentworth said, quietly, "It's decent of you to be concerned, Duncan."

He and Nita hurried across the dining-room and, with inattentive seeming eyes, Wentworth saw Duncan send the gunmen racing along a corridor... a corridor that had an exit on the street! He doubted that it meant an attack. Duncan could not be sure enough of himself as yet. He got into the overcoat he had previously left at the checkroom, hurried Nita out through the doors of the Hesperides. As they stepped out beneath the marquee, a sleek limousine flashed from the curb up the street and swerved to a halt before them. A giant bearded Sikh, his head bound in a turban, leaped from the driver's seat to whip open the door.

Wentworth sprang into the tonneau behind Nita, caught up the speaking-tube as the Sikh, recognizing the need for haste, slid in behind the wheel again.

"Slow just after you turn the corner, Ram Singh," Wentworth snapped. "I'll jump out. Take the *missie sahib* to the apartment, and stay just four minutes. Then drive fast for the address she'll give you."

The Daimler slid powerfully forward and Wentworth whipped toward Nita. In the special rear-vision mirror of the tonneau, he saw the four gangsters of Duncan piling into a sedan behind them.

"They'll follow you," Wentworth said swiftly. "Let them keep you in sight. I'll leave my overcoat and hat here. Rig them up on my cane as if I sat beside you. They won't attack. They suspect where I'm going, and want to keep me in sight. I'll see you in a few minutes. This is the address... Watch Ram Singh on timing. It may be... important!"

Nita's hands clung to his. "Good luck, Dick!" she whispered. "And next time, dear, don't be so careless!" Her tone was light, but Wentworth knew the pain that lurked beneath her words. It was always her way to encourage him.

Wentworth laughed, but his eyes were bitter and cold. "I thought I had to deal with a single case of arson," he said soberly. "There is more behind it than that! I was sure the criminals would hold on to that cigarette-lighter for their own purposes, and was going back for it later. There is a brain behind this, Nita."

Nita's face was set in a smile, but he saw the tightness of apprehension about her mouth corners. "Another battle, Dick?" she asked.

Wentworth's voice was grim. "Before he died, this arsonist—his name was Eggendorfer—talked a little. He said his master's name is... *Munro!*"

Nita's smile was wiped from her lips. She whipped toward Wentworth and her face was frightened. *"Munro!"* she whispered.

BEFORE SHE could say more, the Daimler swerved around the corner and slowed. Wentworth sprang from the running-board and three long bounds hurled him into the shadows of a doorway. The Daimler spurted on and, an instant later, the pursuing gangster car whipped around the corner in pursuit. Wentworth watched them go with grim eyes, his nerves slowly tautening... If he were wrong about their intention... If they should attack Nita... But the Daimler was bullet proof and

Ram Singh was one of the greatest of a great warrior race!

Now....

Cold wind whined desolately along the street and Wentworth, coat collar turned up to hide the white gleam of his formal shirt, felt the bite of the chill, though his blood was racing. This would have to be fast, damned fast! It would be a matter of split-second timing with Kirkpatrick racing to the scene, and his own advantage a matter of seconds only. He could rely on Jackson, but... Why didn't Jackson come?

Why?

His mind flicked back to Nita, racing across the city with those gangsters on her trail. Even she had been shaken with horror at the mention of Munro's name, and she knew him only by reputation. Wentworth had met him once in battle, and the Spider had barely escaped alive from that trap! Munro was damnably shrewd, utterly ruthless, one of the great minds of the criminal world. He....

A battered coupé whipped around the corner with a purring power in the motor beneath the hood that belied the ancient body. Wentworth stepped from cover and the coupé swung in, the door already open. Wentworth leaped in, and Jackson

drove the accelerator to the floor. His hands were white upon the wheel, the muscles ridged out along the broad line of his jaw. More clearly than any words, his tension told how well he recognized the need for haste.

Wentworth was crouched on the floor instantly. He whipped forward the right half of the front seat, and a secret compartment was revealed behind it. No time for the full Spider makeup, but there was a steel mask that he sometimes used in such emergency. It reproduced the Spider's features exactly, but if it should slip, or Wentworth should be captured! With a grim thinning of lips, Wentworth took that risk. Wig, cape, hat… twin automatics.

"Nice timing, Jackson," Wentworth said quietly. "Details!"

"Gave you everything," Jackson's voice had a rasp of taut nerves. "I was at headquarters, according to the Major's instructions, keeping an eye on the commissioner. Told him the Major sent me down to check on records of forgers. Stalled along until this call came in. Headquarters was so upside down I called over Kirkpatrick's own phone!"

"Good work," Wentworth nodded. He was on the seat now, and it was no longer Richard Wentworth who rode beside Jackson, but a hunched and sinister figure, whose eyes gleamed coldly beneath the broad black brim of a slouch hat; whose hands clutched the twin butts of deadly automatics. Damnable having to lose these minutes that might make all the difference between life and death, but he had no choice save to return to Eggendorfer's room as the Spider—and he had been forced to destroy his previous disguise with a vial of acid carried for that purpose.

So far, he seemed to be ahead of the police. He had heard no distant wail of sirens… His keen eyes reached ahead, narrowed as he spotted two men lounging against the front wall of the tenement building that he must enter.

"Shoot past!" he snapped at Jackson. "Then slow on the back street. Those are Duncan's men!"

Jackson twisted about his broad, honest face and there was worry in the eyes that held always a hint of idolatry when they rested on Wentworth's face.

"There'll be a lot of those hoods, Major," he growled. "Couldn't you let me…."

"Just stand by, Jackson," Wentworth ordered quietly. "Usual orders. I'll signal if I need help. Eggendorfer's room is on the third floor, southeast corner."

"Stand by, sir," Jackson acknowledged with a growl, and Wentworth knew that no more was necessary. More than once Jackson had walked into what seemed certain death to serve him….

The car slowed to the curb, seemed barely to hesitate, but when it passed the street light at the next corner, the seat beside Jackson was empty… and on that ominously dark street, a darker shadow had merged with the shadows that cringed against the wall. The Spider moved into battle!

CHAPTER 2
WHERE DEATH WAITS

IN THE dim-lighted room where Eggendorfer lay dead with the mocking crimson seal of the Spider upon his forehead, a gangster stood on guard. In his right fist was a heavy automatic and his eyes roved ceaselessly about the room. Time and time again, he started at some slight creaking in the ancient building. The whine of the cold wind, the tapping fingers of icy snow crystals against the window made him shiver as if with cold. His tongue touched his dry lips and there was fear in the grayness of his cheeks.

He was here because the Spider might return before the police could arrive. Only the threat of death from the boss, the promise of sure support, could have forced him to keep this lone vigil. Suppose the Spider did come!

Mugsy Lugan flinched as a particularly hard gust rattled the loose window. Only the wind… It had to be the wind! Mugsy took a slow step toward the window, shook his head. No, that was against orders. He couldn't even make sure whether it was the Spider. All he could do was stand here and wait… for the Spider. His eyes fell toward Eggendorfer's stiffening body and he flinched. Eggendorfer had waited for the Spider!

Mugsy Lugan shifted his automatic to his left hand, dragged

the right palm against his trouser leg. Geez, sweating in this weather!

"Damn the Spider to hell!" he muttered.

From the window, a voice spoke softly, a mocking voice, flatly metallic and instinct with menace!

"How very inhospitable of you, Mugsy," the voice said, softly. "The Spider is simply paying you a call!"

Mugsy stiffened, and his mouth gaped with the looseness of the fear that ran like ice through all his body. He shivered, turned about laboriously. The gun dangled limply from his fingers— poised on the windowsill, the night cold and black behind him, crouched the becaped and menacing figure of the Spider! A gun glinted in each fist. His eyes seemed to bore like bullets through Mugsy's cowardly flesh. The gun trembled in Mugsy's hand, fell to the floor with a reverberating thud!

"That was wise, Mugsy," came the sibilant mockery of the Spider's voice. "That was very wise! Now pick up that lighter, Mugsy, and bring it to me. And I think it would be advisable for you to hurry!"

One of the Spider's guns lifted an inch, and Mugsy's trembling became violent.

"Yes, sir," he stammered. "Oh, sure, Spider. Right away!"

He bent for the lighter, but his hands were shaking so that his fingers could not clasp it. His face twisted about, warped with fear.

"Don't, Spider," he whispered hoarsely. "Don't shoot. I'm trying. I swear to God I'm trying!"

Wentworth swore impatiently, leaped from the sill. Seconds

were flying, and he could not estimate how many more were left to him. Already, he thought he could hear the faint whimper of police sirens racing to this spot. He took a stride forward, and with a frightened squawk, Mugsy Lugan dodged aside. His hands hit the wall, and he went down on his knees. Wentworth stooped toward the lighter—and hell burst loose in that room!

As Wentworth bent forward, the three doors that opened into that barren room flung wide with whining speed. Dazzling lights converged on Wentworth from those three separate angles—and the doors were crowded with armed men!

"Start shooting!" Mugsy's voice rose, thin with terror. "For God's sake, start shooting. *Kill the Spider!*"

There was that moment's pause while Wentworth stood crouched in the middle of the death-trap; while the blaze of lights pinned him, helpless, against the shadows and the guns of the men in those three doors quested for and centered on his body... and Mugsy pleaded for his death with a frantic certainty that only the quick and deadly fire of his companions could save him from the vengeance of the Spider!

A hoarse oath sprang to Wentworth's lips as he realized the nature of the snare into which he had stepped. Those two men on guard out front had fooled him, that and the call to the police. He had been so certain that the crooks would depend on the police to do their killing for them... and he had walked into this trap.

Wentworth's brain raced madly, seeking a way out. Even the deadly twin automatics of the Spider could not batter a way through this ring of steel. He... the Spider straightened, and the thin lipless gash of the mouth parted. His eyes glared straight into those dazzling lights, and... *the Spider laughed!*

It was a mocking, bitter sound, the laughter of the Spider, an eerie sound in the room's quiet that was the quiet before death. It beat upon the eardrums of the men who faced him, guns in hand for the kill, and it stayed their trigger fingers for that brief fraction of a second. This was the man they had dreaded and feared through endless nights of terror, a superman who always dodged somehow out of their deadliest traps, who rose to kill when they thought him already dead. They had him helpless under their guns and the Spider must know it... Yet the Spider could laugh! The sound of it rasped harshly on their eardrums with a strangely piercing quality.

It was in that heartbeat's pause that the Spider struck! EVEN WHILE he laughed, he was in motion. There was one spot in that room where, for a brief moment, he might be safe... and that was the spot where Mugsy crouched and wailed for the death of the Spider! Not that Wentworth believed the crooks would have any compunction about murdering a companion, if by that means they could achieve the Spider's demise! But they might hesitate... and Wentworth was living by those split-seconds of hesitation.

The Spider had survived a thousand battles by means of those little unheeded heartbeats of time. This second, and the next, and the next... and his laughter had signaled Jackson that he was trapped. He hoped that Jackson had been near enough to hear that piercing, eerie laughter! It might give him the instant he needed to grab the slender length of silk that dangled outside the window, the web by which he had climbed, and could slide to safety again!

As Wentworth took that first long leap, his guns crashed in his fists. They hurled their lances of red flame against the white glare of the flashlights… and two of those lights blacked out! Two men screamed out in mortal agony as the quarter-ton impact of .45 caliber lead drove the fragments of metal and batteries into their bodies!

Before Wentworth could fire again, the guns of the enemy opened up. Their crashing discharge pulsed within his brain, seemed to swell the walls to bursting! The hot lead, flying from three angles, crossed and criss-crossed the spot where the Spider had stood… but he was no longer there! He was a blur of black movement in a room strongly shadowed by the single torch that still blazed from the door. His cape swirled and whipped out from his shoulders until he seemed twice, three times the size of a normal man. He was everywhere at once, and nowhere at all when the bullets flew. The guns in his fists blasted and blasted again—and every bullet sped true! In those crowded doorways, no man could escape or dodge. They were stationary clay-pigeons for the unerring thunder of the Spider's guns!

Two, three seconds beat past in that death-trap, and the Spider's guns had crashed five times. There was a fury of sound, of gun-thunder and human screams, in which individual voice and shot no longer counted. The light in that room of death was red and yellow, the flicker of gunpowder lightning. Only one pair of eyes saw the small sphere that might have been an over-sized baseball lob in through the open window—and the Spider gasped his thankfulness. Every eye saw the flash that came when that sphere exploded there in the middle of the floor beside Eggendorfer's body… and after that they saw nothing at all!

From that burst of flame, darkness spurted across the room, coils of blackness that swallowed even the flashes of the guns; that swirled into the faces of the gunmen and clogged their vision. Wentworth flung himself prone on the floor, and his breath whined in his throat from his furious movements. His lips moved soundlessly, but what he said was, "Bless Jackson!"

His trusty comrade-at-arms had heard his signal laughter, and had hurled a smoke bomb through the window!

In the darkness, the killers were mad with fear. Their guns hammered in a frenzy. Plaster dust mingled with the chemical smoke. Wentworth could hear the thudding beat of bullets jarring across the floor, searching out the walls. Mugsy Lugan had long ago ceased to scream.

Wentworth moved cautiously. His guns were fully loaded again, and even in the welter of battle—the intense darkness which could swallow up even the bitter stab of flame from the guns—he had not lost his uncanny sense of direction. He knew that, beside him on the floor within the reach of his hand, was the corpse of Eggendorfer. Wentworth's lips moved in a faint, mocking smile behind the steel mask of the Spider… and he began to strip off the cape and wig, the black slouch hat, the steel mask itself.

The shooting died away a little; men's voices shouted in fear and questioning. And there was little time. The smoke of the bomb would dissipate presently. Through that lull in the bedlam struck the keening of a police siren, shrieking nearer, nearer....

"Close in!" A man's voice rasped. "Keep bullets going through that window, and close in! We'll rake this room from wall to wall. If that louse is still here...."

And then... the Spider laughed.

"Come, fools!" he shouted. "Come and take me!"

FROM THE darkness, guns roared, and the screams of lead-slashed men lifted terribly. The smoke was thinning, and the flames of the Spider's automatics gave them a target. "There!" shouted the leader. "There against the wall!"

Brilliant flashlights bored once more into the thinning mist of smoke, and the guns bellowed and roared; the walls shook, and the taste of burned powder was in the air, stranglingly thick. There were no more shots from that cape-draped figure against the wall. It shook and quivered to the impact of deadly lead, but still that sinister, changeless face peered out from beneath the hat brim; still it did not flee from their attack!

"He's dead!" the leader said hoarsely. "He's got to be dead! I put almost a whole drum of bullets through him. He... *Come on!*"

Through the darkness they charged. Their guns kicked against their stiffened wrists, and they ignored the dying wail of sirens nearby. To hell with that, if they could kill the Spider! The leader leaped close and slammed the barrel of his sub-machine gun against the side of that lolling head. The black slouch hat tilted up and fell to the floor with a soft little plop, then... then the face of the Spider came loose and fell to the floor. It rang like

28

steel, and they knew it was a mask. But they were not staring at it, they were gazing into the face of the dead man against the wall. A Spider seal gleamed eerily on the forehead.

"Eggendorfer!" the leader shouted. "Damn him to hell, he put his clothes on Eggendorfer and scrammed!"

Laughter came mockingly from behind them, laughter and a swift hail of lead! Men reeled and pitched to the floor. The leader slumped to his knees and his hands clawed at the figure of Eggendorfer, hung by his collar to a light bracket on the wall. They fell together to the floor. Men lifted futile, emptied guns toward the window, but they snapped only at emptiness, at a black rectangle through which swirled a few icy particles of wind-spun snow.

"Beware," came the Spider's voice softly. "Beware, you who would trap the Spider! Carry that warning to… Munro!"

Fear nailed those who remained alive to the floor, and outside the window, Wentworth slid swiftly down the silken rope by which he had climbed, the line that was no thicker than a pencil but which had phenomenal strength, and which the police and criminals alike knew as the Spider's web!

Wentworth hit the pavement, wrapped the silken web into a swift tight ball. Police were hammering into the building now. Those criminals who had survived would not escape, but he had had to cut it terribly fine. Jackson already had gone at his orders. If Ram Singh was late by so much as a minute….

The Daimler careened around the corner, and Wentworth leaped to the street, flung to the running-board as the heavy limousine slowed for an instant.

"Go ahead, Ram Singh!" Nita cried, and slammed the door behind Wentworth. "They're right behind us. Your hat, your coat… Oh, thank heavens, Dick. I heard guns. I never heard so many guns…."

Wentworth dropped back against the cushions and settled his silk hat more smoothly upon his head. His brows were tilted and there was a slight, grim smile on his lips. He saw in the rear-vision mirror that the gangster car had just whirled the corner behind him.

His hand touched Nita's briefly, where they rested on his arm. "I believe I, too, heard… some guns," he murmured. "I fancy there are those who wish… they had not heard them! They won't again!"

NITA'S HANDS clung to his right arm and, left-handed, Wentworth offered a cigarette, snapped flame to the slender platinum lighter that had so nearly brought about his death. By that minute yellow flame, Nita smiled into his eyes.

"Dick!" he smiled. "Showing off at your age! As if I didn't know you had recovered that lighter!"

Wentworth's laughter was tender. This was when Nita showed her true courage. He knew that she had been torn by fears for his safety, but aside from that first involuntary outcry of thanksgiving, she would never admit it. She was easing his own tension now, for none knew better than she that this was only the beginning of the battle—if Munro were involved!

"Tell me, Dick," Nita said quietly. "You mentioned… Munro. I remember… awful things about him." Her shoulders, warm beneath her fur coat, shivered a little.

"No doubt," Wentworth murmured, and his forehead creased. "Munro, the Man of a Thousand Faces! I'd hoped he'd never return to this country! He is probably the greatest criminal organizer it's ever been my misfortune to encounter… and aside from that, a true artist at disguise, hence his name. Munro… The name doesn't mean a thing. He not only can impersonate other people, but he creates a separate personality for each crime. The police hunt him, and find only the shell of the disguise! Never a clue to his real identity. It's his vanity that causes him to use that one name again, after these years. Munro… The fact that he uses it is a taunt and a challenge to me!"

"And this time," Nita said slowly, "Munro's weapon is… arson?"

Wentworth nodded and the last traces of laughter and mockery were gone from his lips, from his eyes. "The man who paid, Eggendorfer, said his boss was Munro. And men who face the Spider in their last hour do not lie!"

"No," Nita said quietly. "I don't think he would lie, but where is the profit, Dick? It's awful to think in terms of profit when human lives are at stake. But that man does! A rattle-trap tenement, and five of those poor children…."

Wentworth's lips were grim. "It is what I mean to find out… tonight!" he said. "And Nita, listen, trust not even a man who seems to be myself from now on, unless he gives you sure proof! It might be… *Munro!*"

Nita whispered, "A password then?"

Wentworth shook his head jerkily as the Daimler slid to a halt again before the Hesperides Club, where a bright neon

31

sign showed three bouncing golden apples. "A password can be faked, my dear," he said slowly. "No one can counterfeit the memories we share!"

Nita stepped down to the curb, her hand in his, and sent her gay silvery laughter into the cold night. "So we can finish out our evening, Dick," she said happily. "That was a foolish mistake…."

The doorman's eyes were fixed on them intently as he swung open the portals of the club and Wentworth knew that Duncan would get a report on Nita's words. The gangster car was just sliding to a halt. The gunman, Mac, flashed across the pavement into a side entrance. When Wentworth and Nita had checked their wraps, Duncan was striding toward them, and there was a frown on his forehead; his dark eyes were secretive beneath veiling lids. And Mac was in the background, his sly face completely puzzled.

Duncan's cordial smile was palpably forced. "I am glad you were able to return, sir!"

Wentworth's smile was affable. "We don't like to leave things half-finished," he said, "and the injury to Miss van Sloan's cousin was a foolish error. A man who looked like Gregory and the doorman of the apartment made a mistake of identity."

"I am complimented that you returned!" Duncan bowed.

Wentworth's brows lifted in mockery. "And I forgot to thank you for the bodyguard, Duncan," he murmured. "I don't know the occasion for it, or is it a service you customarily tender to your clients!"

HE TURNED easily toward Nita, and his eyes swept the corridor. Mac was no longer alone, and he was no longer in the background. He was moving lightly forward, flanked by three other gunmen! The smile on his lips was sly and knowing, and his round pale eyes were eager. Wentworth checked the curse that leaped to his lips.

Had something slipped somewhere? It was part of his plan for the evening to have a showdown with Duncan, to find out where he connected with the death of Eggendorfer, with… Munro! But this was not the time Wentworth would have chosen, with Nita in the very center of it. Wentworth had not even his guns. He had been compelled to leave them, with their incriminating riflings, for Ram Singh to destroy.

"By the way," Wentworth murmured over his shoulder. "When Commissioner Kirkpatrick comes, Duncan, you may show him to our table."

His gaze sought Nita's face, and he saw in the glisten of her eyes that she had spotted the danger. She put a hand on his arm, and leaned close, laughing while she whispered.

"I have a gun in my muff, Dick, if you want to fight!"

He started toward the dining-room—and Duncan stepped into his path.

"I wonder, Mr. Wentworth," he said suavely, "if you would mind stepping into my office a few moments?" His tone was casual, but there was cold menace beneath his voice. At his shoulder, Mac smiled his sly smile.

Wentworth met that smile easily, and welcomed the chance to remove Nita from danger. "If you'll wait for me in the dining-room, Nita," he said. "I'll promise not to be long!"

"I'm afraid we need the lady, too," Duncan said grimly, and

the subterfuge was gone now from his voice. There were three men closing in behind Wentworth. He slid his hands into his trousers pockets and his head was tilted quizzically.

"I've changed my mind, Duncan," he said. "We won't go with you. And if you don't send your trained seals packing at once, it will be my regretful duty to put a bullet through your umbilical. Yes, that protuberance over my trouser's pocket is the muzzle of a twenty-five caliber Colt's. Not a large-caliber weapon, but placed as I have indicated, I think you will find it does the trick, nicely!" Strangely, Duncan smiled. His eyelids lifted, and Wentworth saw there, instead of the fury and frustration he had expected, a gleam of genuine admiration. "Check," he said gently, "you will pardon me now while I make Commissioner Kirkpatrick welcome!" Wentworth turned his head easily and saw the crisply striding figure of Commissioner Kirkpatrick of the police punch in through the main entrance of the club. Sergeant Reams strode briskly at his heels, and there were two other uniformed men. Wentworth laughed… and took his hands out of his pockets. One held his cigarette case, and the other… the slim platinum lighter of the Spider.

"Won't you have a smoke before you go, Duncan?" Wentworth asked lightly.

Duncan hesitated, and looked down at Wentworth's hands. His smile was slight, even pleasant "I'm afraid there isn't time just now, Mr. Wentworth," he said. "If I were you, I would remove the plaster dust from your right trouser leg. It is just possible Kirkpatrick might connect it with… a recent demolition job that the Spider has just finished!"

He strode easily away to meet the commissioner of police and Wentworth bent casually to do as Duncan had indicated, but there was a frown behind Wentworth's eyes, and Nita's hand, touching his, was cold. No question now that Duncan was sure of his connection with the Spider, but what was strange was the man's behavior! Duncan was a big-time gambler, it was true, but he was not of a caliber to meet the Spider on equal terms. Yet he had done just that! More plainly than any words, Duncan had said: *"This is a matter between you and me, Spider. A little private duel we shall finish after a while. I wouldn't want the police to interfere!"*

BEHIND THEM, Kirkpatrick was issuing crisp orders to his men, and Wentworth swung about on his heel, lifted a hand in salute. "You came sooner than I had expected, Kirk," he called, "and I see you've brought extra guests. Good evening, Sergeant Reams!"

The sergeant nodded jerkily. His face was red from the burn of the winter cold, and there was frost in his blue eyes.

"Good evening, sir," he said, "and to you, Miss van Sloan!"

Kirkpatrick strode sharply up to Wentworth, and for once there was no friendliness in his saturnine face. His brilliant blue gaze held no recognition whatever.

"Duncan," he said. "I'll need your office. Bring that hood called Mac. Wentworth, kindly accompany me."

Wentworth shrugged, "I receive the most pressing invitations!" he said comically to Nita. "If you'll wait for me, dear?"

Nita laughed. "Nothing of the sort! I'm coming with you! I'm sure Stanley won't mind, will you, Stanley?"

For once, Kirkpatrick's faultless manners were in abeyance. "As you like, Miss van Sloan!"

He pounded his heels into the soft carpeting as he headed for Duncan's office. Nita's hand rested lightly on Wentworth's arm. The quizzical smile remained on Wentworth's lips, but he wished Nita were out of it. He did not know what evidence Kirkpatrick might have against him, and he could not afford to be slapped into a prison now, even though he might manage to clear himself in trial! Munro would not await his release to press his damnable arsons, for whatever foul profit he derived from it. Human lives were at stake. Beside that fact, nothing in Wentworth's life could be important!

If Kirkpatrick's evidence was strong, Wentworth would have no choice but to make a break for it!

Kirkpatrick was his closest friend, and often they had worked side by side against the bitter enemies of mankind. But Kirkpatrick had long openly suspected Wentworth of being the Spider, though he lacked proof to substantiate that belief. Wentworth knew that if ever his friend did obtain the evidence, he would be treated like any criminal outside the law. Kirkpatrick's allegiance was to society's code of laws—not to an individual's application of justice, however right. So stern was his service to that code that friendship would not weigh against it for an instant.

And Kirkpatrick's manner had served notice that tonight they were not friends; tonight, they were the forces of law—and a man who might be a murderer!

Wentworth seated Nita suavely in Duncan's large, over-furnished office, dropped nonchalantly into a chair himself. He looked up to find Kirkpatrick standing on braced legs in the middle of the office, his face stern above the uncompromising thrust of his jaw.

"Wentworth," he said sharply, "I'll ask you to account for every minute of your evening from seven o'clock to now!"

"An alibi, in fact," Wentworth smiled. "Am I to know of what you suspect me? Ah, well…."

"This is serious, Wentworth!" Kirkpatrick snapped.

Wentworth's face obediently fell into serious lines. "I don't think I care for your manner, Kirk," he said quietly. "I have been here at the Hesperides Club with the exception of a brief trip to my apartment and back. I remained at the apartment between four and five minutes."

"The reason for that trip!"

Wentworth explained casually about the false report that Nita's cousin had been injured.

"It has puzzled me greatly, Kirk," he finished. "No one at all had been injured. The doorman at my apartment, who was supposed to have made the call, denied any knowledge of it. In fact, Kirk, it almost seems that someone wanted to destroy my alibi for precisely that time!"

DUNCAN WAS leaning his hips against the desk, smoking. He smiled, and interrupted. "That undoubtedly explains what I heard, Commissioner," he said. "I heard reports that Mr. Wentworth was to be held up and robbed. I didn't wish him to be annoyed, so I sent along a bodyguard in another car. Except for the few minutes when he was in his own apartment building, they did not lose sight of his car, did you, Mac?"

Mac's face was ludicrous with surprise. He swallowed, tried for his usual sly grin, missed it badly. "That's the truth, Commissioner!" he said. "We followed that Daimler all the way across town and back again, and there he was, big as life, sitting in back with the dame."

Nita's laughter was a trill. "Now, see, Dick," she said. "Why can't you call me interesting things like that? I'm a 'dame!'"

Wentworth's gaze locked with that of Duncan, and once more he was puzzled by the mocking shine of the man's masked eyes. A cold suspicion raced through Wentworth's mind, but when he rose to his feet, it was casually.

"That's very kind of you indeed, Duncan," he murmured. "I wondered at the purpose of the men who followed me. You were one, er... Mr. Mac? Thank you very much indeed."

Wentworth held out his hand, with the adhesive stripped across the back, and shook hands with Mac, then offered his hand to Duncan.

He saw uncertainty touch Duncan's eyes. Kirkpatrick's growl behind Wentworth held relief in its tones. Much as he despised to accept the word of those who lived on the fringes of the law, he felt that Duncan must speak the truth—at least so far as the alibi was concerned—for he knew Wentworth would never enter into a bargain with such a man as this.

"I have my own doubts about the reason for your surveillance of Mr. Wentworth," Kirkpatrick said grimly to Duncan. "You'll overstep yourself someday. I hope soon!"

Duncan's eyes shot past Wentworth to Kirkpatrick, and his voice was mocking. "Mr. Commissioner, it sounds suspiciously as if you were trying to get me to commit a crime so that you could make an arrest! Surely, there are enough crimes in your city already!" As he finished speaking, he accepted Wentworth's handclasp.

Wentworth's eyes bored into the black, cool eyes of the gambler, but they told him nothing. The handclasp did! Once before tonight, he had shaken hands with Duncan, and he knew... *that the man whose hand he shook in this instant was not Duncan!*

A clever artist in disguise might simulate another person so carefully that a casual acquaintance might not be able to detect the difference, but no man could change the bony structure, the shape and thickness of his hand! The hand he shook now was thinner, narrower, with smaller bones. There was something almost feline in the touch!

Perfection in disguise, and a boldness that met the police on equal terms, that dared even to challenge the Spider to a duel.

Wentworth knew, with a terrible certainty, that he was shaking the hand of the man who this night had accomplished, through Eggendorfer, the destruction of a tenement in which five innocent children had lost their lives.

He was shaking the hand of... Munro!

CHAPTER 3
THE SPIDER AT BAY

WENTWORTH'S REACTION to that recognition was instantaneous. Munro was a man who would be gone the moment his hands no longer touched him. Once let him get outside this office, and he could strip off the disguise of Duncan... and vanish! Yet there was nothing, absolutely nothing genuine with which to charge him! He could not say that Eggendorfer, dying, had confessed he had taken his orders from Munro. For it was the Spider who had killed Eggendorfer, and Wentworth could have no knowledge of what the man had said!

Wentworth's mind flashed to Nita, sitting quietly behind him, to Kirkpatrick. If he precipitated a battle now, one of them might be injured, killed. It was characteristic of Wentworth that he did not think of himself, though he was unarmed. But he could not let his fears for Nita stop him. This man was guilty of the murder of five children, and it would not stop there!

Wentworth stepped back and drew a slow breath. He knew that what he was about to say might precipitate a fighting scrape that would kill Nita, but he could not hesitate.

"Kirkpatrick," he said quietly. "This man lies. His men trailed me with intent to kill me. Duncan himself threatened me with guns tonight, and was on the point of taking me a prisoner into his office when you arrived so opportunely. I will swear out a warrant. Arrest this man!"

Duncan's smile did not waver, but something deadly and venomous flashed out of his eyes. He had a cigarette in his fingers and he tapped it gently on the case.

"I submit," he said easily, "that this is scarcely the treatment I would expect in return for an excellent alibi. But, do your duty, Commissioner!"

He held out his wrists, the cigarette still dangling from his fingers. Kirkpatrick grunted with satisfaction.

"I hope you'll stand behind that charge, Dick," he said steadily. "I've been wanting to nail this man. Sergeant Reams...."

Reams took a stride forward, unhooking handcuffs from his belt... and Wentworth uttered a cry and leaped past him. He tried to catch the cigarette that dropped from Duncan's fingers. Too late! The cigarette struck the floor, and exploded! An incredible burst of gray vapor spurted upward from the spot, and in the same moment, the lights in the office blacked out!

Wentworth recognized the gas in the same moment the cigarette exploded. Tear-gas! But he did not check his vain leap. Instead, he hurled himself violently forward, his arms taut to grasp Duncan! A man reeled into him, and Wentworth grappled with him viciously. His powerful legs drove him forward, and he slammed the man hard against the wall! A fist hammered into his chest, and a voice cursed thickly.

"Take that, you rat!" gasped the voice of Sergeant Reams!

Wentworth swore, jerked free, and in the darkness, a man screamed terribly, and then began to strangle in a horrible way. Words tried to bubble through that scream, and they were meaningless, a ghastly sound in the blackness.

"Flashlight, Reams!" Wentworth snapped. "The door, Kirk. I'll take the window. Now, Nita, the lights. Switch behind you!"

An instant after Reams' flashlight snapped across the width of the office, and found nothing, the lights blazed down from the ceiling. Beside the door, Nita was twisted about tensely, her small automatic searching in her fist Guns were in the hands of

Kirkpatrick and Sergeant Reams… and Wentworth was spread across the window. Despite that instantaneous guard, Duncan had vanished! But he had left his mark behind.

Struggling out his life on the floor, hands tearing at the gaping wound in his throat, was the gunman, Mac!

For an instant, the sight held them frozen motionless. Then Nita uttered a gasping cry and turned her face away, buried it in her arms. Wentworth crossed the office in long bounds.

"Whistle up your men, Kirk!" he cried. "There must be some hidden exit to this room—but he'll have to leave the building to escape!"

Kirkpatrick's gun lashed the glass from the window as Wentworth lunged into the hallway. The whistle screamed into the night and Kirkpatrick's deep voice shouted orders, but Wentworth knew in that same moment that it was futile. There were a hundred, perhaps two hundred men in the building—and given ten minutes in seclusion, Munro could easily cast aside the disguise of Duncan and become one of them! He did not even have to disguise himself, for if he appeared in his true identity, no man could recognize him!

WENTWORTH STOPPED his wild dash, knowing in advance that it was futile. Could he shake hands with every man in this place, attempt by that means to identify Munro?

But the man was warned now. Clever as he was, he would find some way to disguise his hands also. Moreover, before he had shaken two hundred hands, Wentworth knew that his own would be so numb that there would no longer be any certainty in his grasp. He was beaten—and once more Munro had left no trail! He had even cut the throat of his private bodyguard, so that the man could tell no secrets! He found Nita leaning weakly against the wall in the hall, still shaken by the awful death she had witnessed. She said, faintly, "Munro?"

Wentworth nodded grimly. "No question about it." He turned toward Kirkpatrick as the commissioner came striding from the office. "It won't do any good to order Duncan picked up," he said quietly. "That wasn't Duncan. I knew it when I shook hands with him, because just a short while ago I shook Duncan's hand. Kirk, my private sources of information in France tell me that Munro has returned to America. That was Munro, in disguise as usual. I am quite sure, Kirk, that these arsonous fires that have sprung up around the city in recent weeks are his work!"

Kirkpatrick gazed keenly into Wentworth's face. "Private information again, Dick?"

Wentworth shrugged slightly, "Call it a hunch, Kirk. Nothing that would hold water in court. If you have no further use for me, I'll take Nita home. She's had… quite a shock."

Kirkpatrick's saturnine face was quiet and very grave. "No, I have no further use for you, Dick, now. I'm sure that Duncan, or Munro, was telling the literal truth. At any rate, the doorman at your apartment could probably confirm the times of arrival and departure. This time, Dick, there is no proof that you are the Spider."

"Ah," said Wentworth, "so that was the reason for the alibi. I'm glad the Spider is operating again, Kirk. Now, there is some hope of catching Munro."

Kirkpatrick shook his head. "Someday, Dick, the Spider will make a mistake!"

Wentworth laughed, "To err is human!"

Kirkpatrick looked at him very steadily. "You will find, Dick, when that mistake occurs, that I have no divinity to grant forgiveness. I am a man with a duty to perform."

Wentworth gripped Kirkpatrick's arm. "No man could wish for a fairer enemy… or a better friend, Kirk," he said quietly.

Kirkpatrick said nothing further, but strode choppily away along the hall. His pace was long, pounding, and there was an aggressive thrust to his shoulders, but there was a touch of weariness, too. He had never fully recovered from that long spell of heart trouble; he had been warned not to work too hard, not to worry. Wentworth felt Nita draw close beside him, and her violet eyes, when he turned to her, were wide and more than a little frightened.

"I'm taking you home, dear," Wentworth said steadily.

Nita's hand tightened convulsively on his arm. "Must you… leave me tonight, Dick?" she said slowly. "Somehow, I… I'm frightened. That man, Munro…."

Wentworth's hand closed hard upon hers. "Munro will not rest," he said simply.

Nita's shoulders shuddered a little, but she said no more.

Against Wentworth's inexorable sense of duty, there was no appeal. Wentworth's brows were creased by a frown. Jackson was certainly somewhere here. He had not been dismissed, and he would not leave Wentworth's trail until that stand-by order was canceled. He helped Nita into her wraps in the lobby. The gaiety went on undisturbed in the Hesperides Club, though police stood beside the exit and each person who left was closely surveyed.

Wentworth quietly donned his own overcoat, drew on white silk gloves. His course was clear. He must find Duncan, the real Duncan, as quickly as possible. That was his one lead, and it might be accomplished as simply as visiting Duncan's home! And that was a task for the Spider....

As they stepped out beneath the marquee, Kirkpatrick spoke from the shadows. "Those two are all right, Reams!"

Wentworth lifted a hand in acknowledgment, but Kirkpatrick did not speak again. The Daimler slid to the curb; the tall turbaned driver leaped out to swing wide the door.

"Drive toward the park, Ram Singh," Wentworth said quietly.

"Han, sahib!"

The Daimler slid smoothly forward and Wentworth watched the rear-vision mirror, and presently when they had gone a few blocks, he saw the battered coupé which Jackson drove swing onto their trail. He smiled, and nodded. Faithful Jackson, still on the job.

"Pull into the curb, Ram Singh!" he called, and turned to Nita.

"Jackson is just behind us, dear," he said. "I'm going to send you home. Better stay at my apartment for the night. It's not the old fortress, but there are still some safeguards. With Ram Singh to watch over you, you'll be safe!"

Nita made no answer, but her arms reached out to him, and the soft sweetness of her lips trembled under his. She smiled faintly as he drew away.

"Don't worry about me, Dick," she said then. "I'm just a bit tired tonight."

Wentworth crushed her to him again. "Don't worry about me, dear," he said. "Only take care of yourself!"

Nita laughed, "Ram Singh will do that for me!"

Wentworth stepped to the pavement, and Jackson's door was already open. He leaped into the coupé, waved a hand, and was gone. Nita leaned back wearily against the cushions as the Daimler surged forward again. She would have preferred to share Dick's peril this night, but she knew that she would only be a burden and hindrance to him. And she could not question his decision that the Spider must once more walk this night, though each minute Dick wore those awesome black robes was fraught with double peril.

NITA VAN SLOAN

NITA CLOSED her eyes and tried to keep her mind off the dangers she knew Dick would encounter before another day was born. She would not sleep, of course… She smiled wanly. It was minutes before a curious thing began to beat its impression into her senses. The tires made a high whining, and she could hear the hissing of a strong wind. Her eyes whipped open, and

47

she saw the buildings were flashing past in a blur. The Daimler was hurtling through the night streets at express-train speed!

"Ram Singh!" Nita cried. "There's no necessity to drive like this. Slow down at once!"

"Han, sahiba!" came the gruff acknowledgment, and the Daimler slowed gradually to a normal speed.

But Nita sat bolt upright in the rear, and a tension of fear crawled along her nerves. *Sahiba!* The word shrieked a warning in Nita's brain. Ram Singh had never called her anything save *'missie sahib'* in all his faithful service. That meant… That meant the man behind the wheel, turbaned and bearded though he was, *could not be Ram Singh!*

But it was worse than that. Not only was the man behind the wheel not Ram Singh, but only one man would be capable of that perfection of disguise—one man who tonight had slaughtered a fellow criminal to close his mouth.

Nita knew with a terrible cold certainty that the man who was supposed to guard her this night, the man who sat so steadily behind the wheel of the car was… *Munro!*

For a space of seconds, while several blocks wheeled past the pulsing Daimler, Nita sat rigidly while something like desperation worked in her breast. She was not afraid. No one who had lived and fought beside Richard Wentworth through the long months of struggle against viciousness could know fear for herself in the ordinary sense. But she was a woman, with a woman's softness, and the man in front of her was a brutal killer who had baffled the police of two continents!

Yet it was not of escape that Nita thought! She was quite sure that Munro was unaware that his disguise had been pierced. If she could think of some way to make him a prisoner and hold him until Wentworth arrived, this latest perilous campaign of the Spider would be finished at its very inception! If only she knew how to reach Dick now!

She did not know his plans….

Nita's hands trembled a little and she pressed them hard together, looked down at them with unseeing eyes. In those narrow, ineffectual hands of hers, she thought, lay the fate of hundreds of people. If she could take Munro prisoner, untold anguish would be saved the people whom Wentworth served… and Dick would not have to risk his life again for a while.

Thought of the fearless man she loved strengthened Nita. She shivered a little and cuddled her hands into her muff as if she were cold… and her fingers closed strongly over the butt of the small automatic she carried there, which Dick had given her and taught her to use expertly! Her movements then were as swift as any pounce of the Spider! Abruptly, she leaned forward and jammed the muzzle of the automatic against the neck of the man behind the wheel.

"Pull over to the curb and stop, Munro," she said, and her voice was coldly incisive. "One false move, and I'll drill that shrewd brain of yours!"

Munro's muscles stiffened against the thrust of that automatic, but that was all. Wordlessly, he slowed the car, and let it roll to a stop against the curb. When that was accomplished, he sat quietly under the wheel for a moment, then a low chuckle rumbled from his chest.

"You are clever, *mamselle,*" he said mockingly. "A fitting mate for the Spider! May I ask... what now?"

"Open the door and step out!" Nita directed calmly. "Keep your hands behind you as you do it. I'm not as good as Mr. Wentworth with this gun, but I'm still equal to a great many men, Munro."

The man obeyed her faultlessly. His left hand pulled the catch, then he put both hands behind him.

"Like this?" he asked solicitously.

Nita made no answer. She had her knee on the back of the seat, ready to slide into the front. Her left hand held a pair of handcuffs, which was among the standing equipment of Dick's cars. Triumph was making her heart beat quickly. She leaned forward to snap the cuffs on Munro's wrists—and suddenly the engine roared, the giant car leaped forward!

Nita squeezed the trigger, but it was too late. The tremendous surge of the motor's power hurled her violently backward from her uncertain perch. She tried to catch herself, to bring the automatic to bear, and the brakes shrieked. Before she could fight against that new thrust of power, Munro was leaning across the back of the seat.

His teeth gleamed evilly through the false black beard, and his black eyes were wide and happy. His hands clasped on her wrists, and he deliberately twisted her gun hand until it was numb with pain; until the gun dropped from her grasp.

"Clever, yes," whispered Munro, his face gloating above hers. "Very clever... but not quite clever enough to trap Munro!"

His palm cracked her hard across the jaw... and before her

reeling senses returned, she was handcuffed and bound, gagged so that she could scarcely breathe—thrown flat upon the floor of the tonneau!

Then the car was speeding forward again, rolling smoothly through the night while its engine droned a song of power. Nita let her head sag forward to the floor, and something like a sob beat against that cruel gag in her mouth; not for herself, but for what her captivity would mean to Dick!

Munro was laughing!

CHAPTER 4
THE FLAME MASTER

THE BATTERED coupé slid quietly through the back streets, boring eastward through the dry. Wentworth was relaxed in the right-hand seat, eyes closed, forcing rest upon himself. For hours he had battled without ceasing, squeezing free from trap after trap. How many had his guns laid low this night, how many had merited the red badge of his swift justice upon their foreheads?

Wentworth's head sagged forward, and he knew that unless he flung himself into fierce action, he was facing one of his spells of black depression. His heart was kind, and if he seemed merciless and ruthless to those who met him on the wrong side of the law, it was because of his stern sense of justice. How many times his unerring guns had spat their lethal lead… and how futile the battle suddenly seemed….

Trouble….

His triumphs came always by herculean effort, and always there was another greedy twisted man waiting to try his skill against humanity—and against humanity's paladin, the Spider! A few minutes before, he had been face-to-face with Munro; now that man had vanished into the nothingness of the air. Where he was now, or in what disguise, Wentworth could not guess… But at least Nita was safe. He could be sure of that, with Ram Singh to guard her!

Jackson's voice was low in his throat. "Flame-extinguishers in a box in the compartment, sir," he said gruffly. "Chemist said they were the most concentrated and effective known. Too expensive for commercial use."

Wentworth lifted his head and a smile moved his lips. Jackson recognized his depression and was trying to stir him from it.

"Thanks," he said quietly. "We'll need them." He opened the compartment, tucked four glass globes into pockets of his cape. "I have an idea that Munro will have at his command ways of setting fires far beyond the knowledge of ordinary arsonists. In his way, he is a genius!"

Jackson grunted, "Maybe. But this time he's bitten off more than he can chew!" Jackson spat out the window.

Wentworth's smile widened at Jackson's fierce loyalty, for he knew that his top-sergeant spoke with complete conviction.

"All you got to do, Major," Jackson went on grimly, "is to find out where these mugs hide out, then turn me and Ram Singh loose on them. That heathen is a dumb guy, but he's pretty handy to have around in a fight. Me and him together…" A smile widened the straight line of Jackson's mouth. "Me, I ain't had a decent fight in months."

He tapped his thick gloved hand on the steering-wheel. Wentworth laughed softly. How could he give way to these foolish depressions when he had the loyalty of men like Jackson and Ram Singh, the love of a fine woman like Nita? If he had doubts of himself, they at least never weakened in their faith!

"It's not as simple as that, Jackson," he said quietly, "but perhaps after I pay this call on Duncan, we'll have an idea where to locate the gang. And then…."

Jackson's mouth opened in a bark of laughter. "Me and Ram Singh!"

Wentworth found himself taut and ready for the battle, and wordlessly, he thanked Jackson. His eyes stabbed ahead. The hard, fine spit of the snow had changed with the dying of the wind. The flakes were larger, and they drifted down across the street lights in a swirling pattern of beauty. The sidewalks glistened wetly.

"Duncan lives in a fourth-floor apartment," Wentworth began quietly, "on the next street over. Two blocks down. I'm going there to have a talk with him."

"Let me side you, Major!" Jackson said eagerly. "There might be some other mugs around!"

Wentworth shook his head, eyes still searching ahead. "You forget, Jackson. You are known as my comrade. And tonight… the Spider walks!"

Jackson shifted impatiently in his seat, but his voice had the flat formality of army service again. "Usual orders, sir?" he asked. "Stand by?"

"Stand by!" Wentworth repeated softly. "The middle of the next block, Jackson. Stay within hearing after you park the car!" INTO THE shadows slid the black sinister figure of the Spider, merging with the iron grating of an alleyway. In his hand, a lockpick of surgical steel glistened for a moment, then the gate swung open. Wentworth closed it softly behind him, flitted silently toward the rear. His eyes quested over the six-story apartment building on the next street, picked out the window of Duncan's apartment. No lights there... The fire-escape would be the quickest way up. There would be few windows opened to this cold.

Wentworth crossed the open courtyard in long bounds, leaped high and caught the framework of the lowest landing. Above him, he heard steel rasp on mortar, heard slats tremble against each other; the entire structure quivered under his smoothly athletic swing and lift that placed him finally kneeling on the platform.

He peered up through the darkness, feeling the wet kiss of snow-flakes on his cheeks, and he swore under his breath. He did not think the sound would alarm anyone. The heavy thrust of the winter wind must be enough to shake this fire-escape! The thing should have been condemned long ago! The owners of these old buildings allowed the bolts and fastenings to rust out; careless fire inspectors permitted them to pass... or their palms were greased!

Wentworth was already on his way up the steps, and his

foot-treads made no sound. So smooth was his progress that even the rattle-trap fire-escape did not rattle. His eyes gleamed coldly. Small wonder that such criminals as Munro could cash in on the weaknesses and hypocrisies of humanity! The owner of this building would receive a Spider-sealed message through the mails, and if it were not heeded....

Wentworth checked at the fourth floor, and peered out toward the window of Duncan's apartment. A narrow ledge ran along the building beneath the windows and, without hesitation, Wentworth stepped out upon it. His shoes dusted off a fine edging of snow. One false step and he would be hurled out into space! Only a man of perfectly controlled nerves, of whip-cord muscles, would have dared that passage—yet Wentworth scarcely thought about it. His mind reached ahead to the room in which he would find Duncan—if Munro had not reached him first! So rapidly he moved, seemingly a black shadow that flitted across the face of the building, that he might have been the very personification of the creature whose name he bore!

Presently, he checked beside a window, and his fingers moved deftly over its facing. The reflected glow of the city sides, always flushed with its myriad lights, reached feebly into the room, and Wentworth nodded as his eyes took in the elaborately over-luxurious furnishings of the place. Expensive—and in wretched taste. Yes, he had been right in his location of Duncan's apartment!

From beneath his cape, Wentworth drew out a device like a doctor's stethoscope and fastened a suction disk to the window-pane. The glass acted as a huge diaphragm, picking up every sound within the room. There were muffled footsteps, but from their faintness, Wentworth knew they were in the hall beyond the door. There was another muted, regular sound, and then the jiggle of bed-springs. Wentworth's smile was grim on his lips, as he thrust the instrument away. Duncan was at home!

His hand closed on the window frame and, soundlessly, it slid upward in its grooves. The Spider's skill held it from vibration. Heat swirled out into his face, and the stale bite of whisky. Effortlessly, the Spider slid over the sill, and now he was a crouched figure of menace, looming enormous in the black cape.

There was the glint of gun-metal in his fist, and his feet made no sound as he slipped across the drawing-room toward what he knew must be the bedroom entrance. The door stood open. The sound of breathing came to him again, and once more the threshing of bed-springs. So much the better, if Duncan were awake!

Wentworth slipped a small flashlight from his pocket and, muffling it beneath his cape, he stared fixedly at it through a long moment while his eyes adjusted to the brightness. Then he stepped into Duncan's room… and swept on the lights.

"Good evening, Duncan!" he said quietly. "Such a polished gentleman as yourself should rise when he has a visitor!"

His eyes were burning toward the bed. He could see the figure beneath the bed-clothing, covers drawn even over the head. There was a renewed, frenzied threshing of the bed-springs. The covers jumped and surged... but the man did not sit up as Wentworth bade him! A sharp oath sprang to Wentworth's lips. In a single long bound, he reached the bed, whipped the covers back.

There was a man in the bed all right, a man with a bristling black beard parted by the tight white bonds of a gag. Black eyes glowered fiercely up into his.

Wentworth gasped, *"Ram Singh!"*

It was no more than a glance and a beginning of a word that he uttered, and then Wentworth did a curious thing! He hurled his entire body forward and flung himself face down across Ram Singh's body, and whipped his cape up over his own head. At the same instant, the room exploded into flame!

IF WENTWORTH had been one instant late in his swift leap, those flames would have seared the life from his body in that first flash! As it was, he felt the hot bite of the knife-points of flame, heard the window crash out with the force of the concussion! No ordinary man would have lived through that first split-second of disaster, but Wentworth would not have this long survived his fierce battles with crime had he not been a little greater than human.

In the instant when he was whipping aside the covers, to gaze at the incredible fact that Ram Singh was a bound prisoner in Duncan's bed, Wentworth's all-seeing eyes had caught sight of another thing. He had glimpsed a wire, so fine as to be invisible except on close inspection, fastened to the bed-clothes. He had felt that wire catch and drag as he flung the covers aside. More than that had not been necessary! He was on the trail of an arsonist, and such men dealt in flame-traps!

Wentworth tried to roll Ram Singh from the bed, but ropes held him prisoner. Wentworth's hand stabbed beneath his cape and brought out... the glass globes of the flame extinguisher! Fiercely, he hurled one where the red, leaping flames were hottest! Already, the fire was beginning to roar with the draft from the open window. The rug, walls, even the bed itself, was alive with little dancing blazes! Then the extinguisher burst!

Where it shattered against the wall, the flames leaped fiercely high... and went out! White fumes crawled along the floor, and where they rolled, the spots of fire pinched out like a match tossed into a basin of water. One more of the extinguisher bombs Wentworth hurled, and the last of the blazes was blackened. The room was completely dark now. Plainly, the wiring system had been involved in that touch-off; was blown out now!

Wentworth thrust himself violently from the bed, and a keen pocket-knife flicked open in his hand. He worked with furious speed, slashing loose the bonds that held Ram Singh. Even after that so short blaze, the air of the room was stifling hot. It reached with tearing hands into his lungs. The fumes of the extinguisher crawled close to the floor, but Wentworth coughed stranglingly as he worked... His mind raced even faster than his deft hands.

No question that Munro had come before him, exactly figuring the Spider's next step; no question either that this flame-trap was only the beginning! There would be killers here whose job it would be to make sure of the Spider's death! At any moment, the doors might crash in, the gunmen hurl themselves to the attack! Ram Singh must be free then....

These thoughts were in the forefront of Wentworth's mind, but there was a nagging agony there, too, that he would not permit to make itself felt. Ram Singh's presence here could mean only one thing: he had been overpowered by some trick while Wentworth and Nita had been inside the Hesperides Club the last time. And that meant... that meant the man who had driven Nita away in the Daimler was *Munro!*

Wentworth ripped the gag from Ram Singh's lips. "Quiet!" he warned. "There will be enemies near!"

Ram Singh heaved his broad-shouldered length from the bed, and Wentworth caught the gleam of his teeth as he spat on the floor. *"Wah,"* he rumbled softly. "Thy servant is a swollen-bellied idiot from the hills! They tricked me, *sahib!* Thy servant is unfit to live!"

Ram Singh was suddenly on his knees before Wentworth, and his powerful hands ripped open the throat of his tunic.

"Master," he growled, "they have taken my knives, else I would spare thee the task! Slay a dog who is unfit!"

Wentworth's hand dropped heavily on Ram Singh's shoulder. His own heart was lead in his chest "If you deserve death, my warrior," he said in the harsh Punjabi that was Ram Singh's native language, "then I also deserve that fate. For I rode behind this man, clothed in thy garments! And I did not know him! I did not know him... and he carried off... the *missie sahib!*"

A growl of rage rumbled in Ram Singh's chest. He was suddenly on his feet, and his crouch was like a beast. His hands swung restlessly. "Master," he whispered, "let us, thou and I, earn the right to live! When I have found those who hold the *missie sahib*...."

Wentworth's own lips were curved in a wintry smile. He heard a few frightened calls in the courtyard outside the window, but on this floor, there was complete silence. And it was a silence of waiting, and of death!

"That door leads into the hallway, Ram Singh," he said. "It is locked! And our enemies are outside!"

Ram Singh crossed the room in two easy strides, and his hands clamped on the knob

Ram Singh was a bound
prisoner in Duncan's bed.

of the door. His shoulders, his back arched like the bow of a catapult.

"I will want one man alive," Wentworth's whisper ran.

There came a slow creaking from the door. Ram Singh's breath exploded in a curse from his lips... and suddenly he straightened. There was a ripping of wood, the scream of torn metal! Ram Singh wrenched the door from its hinges! A hoarse shout burst from his lips. He thrust the door before him, and lunged out into the hallway!

THE ENEMY was waiting, men at each end of that narrow hallway with guns in their fists. They were waiting... but they were not ready. So swift was Ram Singh's leap that he was half-way to the nearest men before they realized their prisoner had burst from the apartment! Ram Singh whipped the door above his head, and his teeth gleamed amid the thicket of his beard. The war cry of his native hills roared joyously from his throat! A single gun spat then, wildly, and Ram Singh hurled the door, like a broad-bladed javelin, at the killers! A man turned to run, and the door caught him in the small of the back, bent and broke him; carried him on against his fellows crowded in that narrow corridor! Three men went down, and Ram Singh shouted again and leaped through the air, with his great fists reaching before him! All that Wentworth saw as he flung through the doorway, and afterward he ignored the men at Ram Singh's end of the corridor. He had his automatics in his fist and he pivoted to the right—began shooting!

There were five men at his end of the hall. One of them, straight ahead, grasped a machine-gun. Out of doors on either side of the hallway leaned the other four, and revolvers were in their fists. In that single sweep of his eyes, Wentworth placed them all, estimated them—and his guns, hard-pressed against his hips, jerked in the first salvo of death!

His first bullet caught the crouching machine-gunner squarely in the forehead and whipped him backward out of sight through that darkened doorway. His weapon clattered to the floor and, afterward, his feet showed. They drummed the floor for a little while. But Wentworth was scarcely aware of that. The guns throbbed like living things in his fists, scoring along the walls as they skimmed toward those twin doorways from which death threatened. A gunman lurched backward against his companion, surged forward again as the other opened panicky fire on the Spider—and hit his own partner instead!

Another man, drilled through the shoulder, was whirled out into the middle of the hallway by the sledge-hammer of the Spider's lead. He pitched to his hands and knees and began to scramble frantically, crazily toward that dark doorway where the machine-gun lay. There were only two men left alive in those doorways, and they had flinched back out of sight.

Wentworth heard Ram Singh's pantherish stride behind him. "What, master," he jibed, "are there still men alive down here?"

Wentworth's smile twisted his lips. He was waiting while the crawling gangster grappled for the machine-gun. His eyes flicked to those two empty doorways.

"Throw a body down the hall," he murmured, and Ram Singh laughed harshly. His breath gusted out through his nostrils and, over Wentworth's head, sailed the limp-armed body of a man.

It crashed to the floor before the doors, and flame spat out of the darkness. Wentworth squeezed each trigger once, and there was the concerted clatter of falling guns within those rooms. He had had only the gun-wrists of the men to shoot at—but he had needed no more target than that!

There were screams inside those rooms, pain and fright hoarsening the voices. And the gangster with the broken shoulder had his machine-gun.

"Drop it, fool, and live," Wentworth sent his harsh whisper sibilantly through the hallway.

The man's jaw was chattering with fear. His eyes strained wide and blind in his face. Perhaps he could not hear! His hands shook as he tried to bring the machine-gun to bear. Wentworth squeezed a trigger, and the machine-gun leaped like a living thing from the man's hand.

"Take him, Ram Singh," Wentworth whispered. *"Alive!"*

With a shout, Ram Singh bounded down the hallway. Wentworth moved forward more slowly. A glance behind him showed what fearful carnage the bare hands of the enraged Sikh had performed. There no longer were any cries from the two rooms that flanked the hall, yet there should be wounded men in them. There should be....

Wentworth stiffened to gauge the screams and shouting that echoed through the building. Undoubtedly, the police already had been summoned. He couldn't have much time. But why were those two men in the dark rooms silent? Wentworth's eyes narrowed in abrupt alarm. He leaped through the nearest doorway and flung the strongly concentrated beam of his pocket-flash about the room. *Empty!* A bound took him across the hallway and into the opposite room. That also was empty, and ropes swung from the window!

Through a long moment, Wentworth stood there staring out into the darkness from which the snow whirled like dark specks against the sky-glow, and then a shout lifted to his lips. He wheeled out of the room.

"Bring the prisoner, Ram Singh!" he shouted.

HE PLUNGED for the steps, toward the screams and the shouting below him. No question what those escape ropes meant. They had not been left there for the killers to escape from the Spider. Munro had never expected the Spider to emerge alive from Duncan's room; nor would he have provided for his men to escape. Nor would they have needed the ropes for escape, if the fire in Duncan's apartment had spread. But if this apartment building were set for a touch-off, if the flames were meant to leap up this unguarded wooden stairway and sweep the building in one terrifying holocaust of destruction—then they would have needed those ropes, and needed them badly.

Wentworth took the stairs in great bounds. "Fire!" he shouted, as he ran. "Fire! The building is on fire! Get out! Get out fast— before it's too late! Hurry!" Voices muted beneath the lash of his voice. In the dim-lighted hallway below him, white faces turned up toward him. An old woman with a white cap upon her whiter hair smiled uncertainly with wrinkled lips, and a girl in a feathered negligee tossed her head, and smiled a little slyly. There was a man in trousers and undershirt, and he stared at Wentworth with spreading eyes. His red face drained of color.

"*The Spider,*" he whispered, and his voice broke. He screamed, "*The Spider!*" He turned and began to tear down the steps. They shook under his terrified tread!

Wentworth swung his arm at the people gathered there in a tight, terrified bunch. "Come on!" he shouted. "Follow me! I tell you the house is on fire!"

He stampeded down the steps behind the man, hearing his screams run ahead of him, hearing the terror that the mere mention of the Spider's name could spread in the sudden stillness; and the sudden screams that followed in the wake of the man's flight. Wentworth's lips were grim. He could not blame the people for fearing him, though it was in their service he had done—what he had done. They could not reason out his motives. They only knew that many had been found dead with the glittering red mockery of the Spider's seal upon their forehead. And so they feared....

It was a glancing thought across Wentworth's mind as he raced for the first floor. He could do no more than shout a warning to the people he passed. It was on the first floor, in the basement beneath, that he must seek to prevent this threatened holocaust. The touch-off mechanism would be there; the naphtha to spread the flames instantaneously. God, if only Munro were here now! Wentworth's fists tightened in white hammers at his side! The damnable callousness of the man to set such a trap, when scores of human beings were clustered in these ancient buildings; when every fire he touched off meant human lives! But he would not care for that, only for money in his pocket, by whatever scheme he used to collect on these pyres of the living.

THE SPIDER AND THE FACELESS ONE

As he ran, Wentworth heard a sound pierce through the beat of terror that raced about him. The shriek of speeding police sirens! His teeth locked together. They would be here within instants, and all about the street echoed to screams that blazoned the name of the Spider! Immediate flight was the only thing that could save him. He had his prisoner. Ram Singh could force words from the man, if the fear of the Spider would not. Within his grasp was the means to smash Munro!

But Wentworth did not even hesitate on the first floor, where he might have dashed to safety. He swung down the narrow hallway, batted open the basement door. He had to save these people first of all. If he could find the touch-off mechanism in time! He knew he had not many seconds. The precipitate flight of those gunmen told him that. He peered down into the blackness of the basement, and the hot volatile stench of naphtha struck across his nostrils. Even as he started down the steps, he saw the hot leap of an electric flash!

A shout rose in Wentworth's throat. He hurled himself backward, slammed the door, dodged aside. A rumbling concussion made the floor leap beneath his feet. The basement door was torn from its hinges, and jagged swords of red flame stabbed out through the opening! There was that moment's pause, and then flame was boiling out through the doorway, as coffee boils over from a pot. Gouts of red and yellow rolled across the floor and where they touched, fresh fire leaped up to add to the billowing folds of pure flame.

Wentworth picked himself up from its path and staggered toward the front of the building. Men and women were scream-

67

ing, throwing themselves from the first-floor windows. Two or three streamed down the steps and out the front door, but already the flames were working on those wooden stairs, dancing joyously, bubbling through the cracks, spreading… Halfway down the first flight, Ram Singh was crouched with the unconscious gangster across his shoulder. Escape was easy now. The police had not yet arrived.

It was like the Spider that he did not hesitate at all. On the one hand was safety in escape; on the other death either by fire or at the guns of the police. But human lives were at stake, the people whom the Spider served selflessly and without stint!

Wentworth did not think of escape. He thought of an old woman in a nightcap, and a saucy young girl; he remembered the frightened wail of children.

"Out, Ram Singh!" he ordered. "Save yourself, and take the prisoner to the car!"

And the Spider whirled and bounded up the stairs, back into the teeth of flames—into the mouth of hell!

CHAPTER 5
THE MOUTH OF HELL

WENTWORTH RACED furiously up the steps, toward the surge of people who fought to descend that narrow, treacherous way. Wentworth felt the stairs tremble violently under his tread. A step cracked and collapsed under the thrust of his foot, and up the well, a tower of flame flapped in sudden fury. It twined its hot arms across the stairs and Wentworth hurtled it with a muffled shout.

The heat stabbed into his lungs and he staggered.

Instantly, a strong arm was about his shoulders, heaving him upward. And in his ear, the calm voice of Ram Singh spoke gravely.

"Your orders, *sahib!*"

Ram Singh had chosen to die beside the master he loved rather than seek safety in flight!

Wentworth whirled toward the valiant Sikh and the screams of terrified humans beat about them like a leaden hail. A man ran at the flames on the steps, shrieked and hurled himself headlong through the licking tongues. His body struck with a crash, and there was a rending, tearing sound! The steps gave way beneath him, and his scream soared, but the flames' roar drowned it quickly. They leaped higher, released by the fall of the stairs.

Wentworth's lips moved in a slight smile of acknowledgment of Ram Singh's courage. He thrust out his hand, pointing.

"Drive the people upstairs!" he ordered fiercely.

He flung up his arms, and in the hot draft of the flames, his cape billowed out behind him like black wings, a brave erect figure against the scarlet and yellow of death that flared behind him.

"Up!" he shouted above the flame-roar. "Climb upward! The roof is your only protection! Fire-engines are coming with ladders! Get up!"

He yelled.

A few women fled before him toward the stairs, but there was terror above, and people fought also to run down that narrow treadway to what they hoped was safety. Ram Singh reached over the rail and seized a man by the neck, dragged him from the steps.

"Up!" he shouted. "Go up!"

His scowl was fierce, and the women broke before him and fled upward. At the head of the steps, they ran into a jam of human beings. Wentworth leaped for the stairway and his legs drove him fiercely. His hands reached out over the heads of the terrified people and picked out the cowards—the men who fought blindly and crazily to escape, and were imperiling other lives. Wentworth struck crisp, reaching blows. The men went down, and the jam was broken. Afterward, the people could move more swiftly.

They were on the third floor now, and already the heat here was incredible. Black smoke swirled and drifted through the hallways, and there were strangling gasps of terror. A woman was on her knees with a baby in her arms, and two other children clinging to her, big-eyed with fear, too frightened even to cry.

"The fire-escape, Ram Singh!" Wentworth said quietly. "Get back there and see that there is no fighting."

Ram Singh tossed his prisoner to the floor and darted back through the wide-open doorways toward the fire-escape and Wentworth heard his voice ring out fiercely, batter down the panic screams. Wentworth bent over the woman with the children, and she flinched from his touch.

"It will be safer up above," Wentworth said gently.

70

The woman cringed away, rising to her feet. She turned and ran toward the steps upward, with the children clinging to her.

"Who's the funny man, Mother?" the little boy piped. "What are you running for, Mother? He's a nice man...."

Wentworth ranged swiftly through the rooms of the floor, and found it deserted. Most of the people here had made their escape by the stairs, or already had fled before him up the steps. Ram Singh stood braced outside a window, and his great right fist was lifted like a mallet.

"You walk slow," he shouted, "or by Kali, I will smash heads!"

Wentworth stared out the window. The fire-escape was jammed with human beings, creeping, fighting their way downward, and Wentworth felt the blood drain from his heart at the sudden memory of the weakness of that fire-escape, and how it had rattled and swayed beneath his single weight!

"Come, Ram Singh!" he shouted. "For God's sake, hurry!"

He whirled and darted out into the hallway. The heat struck him like a solid wall, and he bent his head, muffled his face in his cape and plunged on. A tongue of flame lashed across his ankles like the bite of a scourge. He made the steps. There was no one on it now; no one at all. He plunged upward and felt the creaking of the stair beneath his feet, felt the blistering intensity of the heat that roared up this open stairway.

"Up another floor!" Wentworth shouted. "Make the people go on that fire-escape slowly, not more than twelve at a time! It's weak. May break!"

He darted toward the fire escape and Ram Singh's huge

hand clamped on his shoulder. "You go upstairs, master," he said simply. "I stay here!"

Wentworth whirled, and his gray-blue eyes flashed with pale fire. "Obey!" he bit out.

Ram Singh stepped back under the fury of those eyes, and touched his hands to his forehead in low salaam. Without another word, he whirled and sped toward the steps. Wentworth plunged on toward the room which held the fire-escape exit.

NO LIGHT burned within the room, but none was necessary. All outdoors seemed one scarlet tower of light. The flame-glow blazed in through the window as from the mouth of a furnace. At the window, a dozen men and women fought and brawled like animals to escape. A man struck about him fiercely with his fists. The woman with the baby in her arms pitched to the floor, a girl screamed as she was hurled half across the room. Immediately she was on her feet again, and dashing back into the mêlée! The man won a moment's freedom there at the window, got half-way out. Another man seized him by the shoulders and hurled him back… and no one climbed out at all!

Wentworth whipped out an automatic and fired a shot into the ceiling. "Stop fighting," he ordered coldly, "The first person who strikes another dies!"

He strode toward the window, and suddenly here was a thing among them that they feared more than the scarlet caress of the flames. Here was a terror with a gun in his fist. One man lifted himself slowly from the floor, and suddenly flung headlong at Wentworth!

Wentworth stepped easily aside, and the gun lifted and fell… and the man was sprawling on the floor, unconscious.

"Now then," Wentworth's voice was quiet, even calm. "Women and children first!"

He picked up the woman with the baby, and her eyes lifted to his face… and this time she did not cringe. A hesitant smile moved on her lips and Wentworth helped her toward the window… but he did not turn his back on the others. He swung the children to the fire-escape platform after their mother. Above him, he could hear the harsh rasp of Ram Singh's voice… and there were not many on the fire-escape.

"Move swiftly, but without running," Wentworth called to the people on the fire-escape. "This thing is weak!"

The little boy was grinning at Wentworth, "Good-bye, funny man," he said, and toddled down the shaking metal steps.

One by one, gun bitterly ready in his fist, Wentworth issued the people to the fire-escape. His eyes quested beyond the immediate group. Against the wall, he saw the old woman with her white, white hair. Beside her, a small, withered mouse of a man stood quietly.

"Come, mother!" Wentworth called.

The woman's withered lips smiled, "Let the young ones go first," she said. "They have so much to live for…."

The little man beside her took the old woman's arm and urged her forward.

"Take care of her," Wentworth told him gently.

The man's eyes were large behind his glasses. "If you don't

mind," he said, his voice thin and reedy. "I think I'll wait a while. I never could stand heights."

Wentworth stared at him, but there was no time for argument. He swung the woman from the floor, set her gently on the platform. In the red light below, he could see firemen darting into the court.

"There will be help below," he told her.

The woman's withered hand clung to his for an instant. "Bless you, Spider," she quavered.

Wentworth swung then on the huddled men, crouching to one side of the window under the threat of his guns. They were racked by coughing from the fumes that seeped through the closed door, and there was hatred in their eyes.

"One at a time," Wentworth told them grimly. "I'll be at the window above you. The first man who hurries, or tries to rush the others… I'll shoot! All right, easy now!"

They went out of the window on their hands and knees, and they did not hurry, or fight. Wentworth saw their faces turned up, rosy in the firelight… and then it happened!

With a rending sound of tearing metal, a bolt ripped out of the bricks, and one end of the platform swung clear of the wall. There were shrieks and wild shouts below. Men started to run down the slanting ladders and up above Ram Singh's voice lifted in a hoarse shout!

Wentworth flung a single shot downward, and shouted a warning. He clamped an arm inside the wall then, and locked the other about the rail of the swaying platform. By an exertion of his utmost strength, he tugged it back against the building!

"Ram Singh!" he shouted, and his voice was hoarse with strain. "Ram Singh… *hold up the fire-escape!*"

There were sudden groaning sounds of wrenched iron, and another bolt gave way. Wentworth's back bowed with effort. His head sagged downward, and his teeth set in his lip. The iron seemed to be severing his arm, his muscles were strained to breaking. Vision swam before his eyes. He was aware of shouts beneath him. The people below realized their danger, and were rushing pell-mell down the metal steps. Those still above them… and there was another floor above Ram Singh… saw their last means of escape eluding them and stormed the windows in a mass. They crowded the platforms to overflowing. They fought to get down the stairways.

And the arms of two men alone anchored that mass of steel, those struggling people to the wall! Wentworth could feel fresh weight sagging upon him. He heard the ripping tear of his coat across his shoulders as the bulge of his muscles swelled against it. Thinly, he heard a man's voice beside him, a squeaky, thin voice that repeated one sound over and over again. It was desperate, that voice, and Wentworth remembered the mouselike little man who would not leave.

"Web!" he cried. "Your *web!* Where is it?"

From great depths, Wentworth heard and recognized the words and could not seem to answer. It was a violent effort of will even to remember where he had tucked the powerful line of silk that was his web. Somehow, he forced out words, dragged from the bottom of his mind. So great was the strain upon him that he could not even be sure that the man's hands touched his body, but presently the man was shouting at him again.

"Not good at knots!" he cried. "Think it will hold!"

Wentworth lifted up his head as a man will drag a great rock from the earth, and turned it toward the fire-escape. The silken web had been twisted between a steam pipe inside, and the metal frame-work of the fire escape. It was doubled and redoubled a dozen times... and as the little man said, the knots were peculiar, but it looked as if it would hold!

WENTWORTH LIFTED his head heavily and gazed up at Ram Singh. There were only a few people left on the fire-escape, and they were running down the steps toward him. They went past with frightened glances at the man in black. If they noticed that the cords stood out like ropes in his neck, that his face was fiery with congested blood and effort, they said nothing.

Woodenly, Wentworth's eyes followed them downward as they fled, saw firemen snatch them from the last rungs and rush them clear of the wavering metal deadfall. Wentworth lifted his eyes to Ram Singh and the Sikh's eyes were bulging in his head with effort.

His voice reached down to Wentworth feebly. "Go down, master," he called, "and then I...."

"Let go!" Wentworth called. "Let *go!*"

His sharp command penetrated even the lethargy of utter fatigue that gripped Ram Singh, and he saw the mighty arm of the Sikh loosen its hold. He let go in the same instant. The metal frame-work swayed out from the wall. A final bolt snapped up near the roof... and then with a rush, the whole fire-escape plunged down into the courtyard! The uppermost platform struck first, bounced high, and then it was all over. A heap of twisted scrap-iron lay in the courtyard.

Somehow, Wentworth dragged himself back inside the window. His web still dangled there, looped about the steam pipe. The rusted iron of the fire-escape had given way first. Slowly, Wentworth unwound the web. He was realizing that it might make the difference between life and death for them now. He pushed out from the wall, and the little man smiled at him hesitantly.

"I hope I tied it all right, Spider," he said.

Wentworth felt laughter prod at his chest. He dropped an arm, a weary, strained arm, about the man's shoulders. "No giant could have done better," he said.

The little man flushed and hung his head, and Wentworth strode with him toward the door. He pressed a palm against the door, flinched at the heat of it; stepped back.

"No man could live out there now," he said. "Even to open that door would mean we would be instantly suffocated by superheat."

With long strides, he returned to the window. Ram Singh was leaning out.

"There are still fools upon the roof, master!" Ram Singh called, "and the ladders cannot reach them because of the flames!"

Wentworth felt a dizziness that was exhaustion sweep through him, but he shook his head vehemently and reached out with the coiled web.

"Catch!" he called, and flung the line upward.

Ram Singh's hand wrapped about the silken line and Wentworth turned to the small man beside him.

"You're going out, now!" he said quietly. "There's no more you can do here!"

The man shook his head stubbornly, eyes big behind the glasses. "I'm not a leader," he said. "Very few of us are born to that... but I can follow! You may need me on the roof!"

Wentworth choked back an impatient exclamation, looped the rope beneath the man's arms. "This time," he said grimly, "you lead! *Haul away!*"

The man hung passively in the loop while Ram Singh threw his great muscles into the task. Wentworth twisted away from the window. They had lost the prisoner that Ram Singh had taken, but this was the fourth floor where Duncan's men had tried to trap him. That door in the side wall... Wentworth leaped to it, and slapped his palm against the wood. It was hot, but not like that one which opened into the hallway. He wrenched it open, and black smoke fanned into his face!

Wentworth strangled, threw the cape over his head, and plunged into the heat. Even through the thickness of his cape, he could sense the red leap of flames. Suddenly, he tripped and fell. His hands plunged against the body of a man! Cautiously, Wentworth uncovered his face, and recognized one of the killers!

With a quick surge of strength, Wentworth caught up the body and hurried back to the room he had quitted. Ram Singh's shout was anxious, and Wentworth leaned out the window to reassure him, caught the silken line as it snaked down again.

Rapidly, he secured it about the man's body, then he went up the silken line, feet braced against the wall, hauling in hand-over-hand! The instant his feet struck the floor inside the window upstairs, he whirled toward Ram Singh.

"Dead man on the other end of the line," he snapped. "Bring him to the roof! Where's that little man?"

Ram Singh's lips moved in a grin. "On the roof," he grunted. "He talks too much."

Wentworth grinned back slowly in Ram Singh's eyes, recognizing the admiration of the Sikh. Then Wentworth loped across the room. The air was a little clearer here, but it would not last long. The wood of the floors was beginning to smolder... He sprang for the stairs, and raced to the roof, heard Ram Singh's heavy tread behind him. On the far corner of the roof were six women, huddled together, and over them stood the little man, looking out very quietly into the night. There was another building over that way, a good fifty feet away. There was nothing else. WENTWORTH RAN toward him, ducking under the mess of radio aerials that criss-crossed erratically; heard Ram Singh hurl the body to the roof and pound after him. In a swift instant, Wentworth leaned over the balustrade and surveyed the scene below. The flames billowed out from the windows, and even at this height, the heat was unbearable. No, no ladders could reach them here. He made a swift circuit of the roof. On one side, there was a two-story building, and there were few windows on the wall. As yet, the fire had not broken through.

Instantly, Wentworth's plan was formed. He sprang atop the balustrade, and his cape billowed out in the rising heat from

79

the flames. He cupped his hands to his mouth and sent a clear shout ringing toward the streets below. Even above the roar of the flames, the answer came back. It was a sigh, a groan of a hundred, a thousand voices.

"The Spider! The Spider!"

Wentworth lifted his hands for silence, and once more called out: "Roof to the left! Spread nets!"

There were long moments of uncertainty while Wentworth repeated that call and then he saw firemen stream out onto the roof! But already, it threatened to be too late! A section of the brick wall had fallen, and the flames licked out furiously! The firemen could not come close enough for the people to jump. Wentworth saw men in the white asbestos suits of the smoke-eaters run in their heavy burdened way toward the building, but knew they would come too late.

He cupped his hands. "Here they come!" he shouted. "Ram Singh… *Throw them!*"

The women screamed, began to run like frightened fowls about the roof. It was the little man who stepped forward then. His face was white as the face of the high-sailing moon, and there was a quaver in his voice.

"I'm a fool about heights!" he said, and swallowed hard. "B-but you can throw me!"

The women stared then, and one of them came forward. "If he makes the net," she said, "you can throw me!"

Another woman darted forward. "No, no, throw me first! They can't hold the nets this near very long!"

Wentworth smiled thinly at the little man, "So you can't lead?" he asked softly.

He nodded to Ram Singh, and the giant Sikh caught the woman at the hips and whirled her high over his head. He ran toward the balustrade, and… hurled her into space! Her scream soared up into the heavens, and the white faces of the other women lined the balustrade. But Ram Singh's cast was true, and the woman smacked into the net… and was taken out safely.

Swiftly then, Ram Singh and Wentworth hurled the others. The last one they both had to swing between them, like an adagio dancer by hands and feet, before she could be hurled into a high arch toward the net. She just made the edge of it, and afterward, the firemen shrank back. The flames were boiling out.

Wentworth whirled toward Ram Singh and together they gazed out over the fiery abyss. A reedy voice spoke into their silence. "It's too far to throw me," he said. "Too bad!"

Wentworth turned quickly, and he had the silken web in his hand. "With this, we can make it," he said quietly, and knotted the web beneath the man's arms. He lifted them submissively, but his eyes were very wide. He took off his glasses and his hands were trembling.

"I don't like to go first," he said. "Suppose the web catches fire when you lower me through the flames?"

Wentworth put his hands on the man's shoulders, looked him directly in the eye. "We're going to swing you clear of the flames," he said. "If we never meet again, I want you to know this: I've never met a braver man!"

The little man flushed and dropped his eyes. "Why—why, Spider..." he began.

He had not chance for more. Ram Singh caught him up in his arms and ran toward the end of the roof. Swiftly, they lowered him and then Ram Singh and Wentworth together began to swing him. He hung limply in the bight of the rope, a little man afraid of heights, a little man who knew he would never be a leader. At first, he moved so very little, then his body began to sweep through a slow arc, faster, faster... Back and forth across the rear of the building they swung him, until his body was sailing out beyond the side wall, out toward the net that was spread on the adjacent roof.

"Now!" Wentworth gasped.

As the man's body swung again to the farthest limits of the web, they let it rush out between their hands. Wentworth had the end twisted around his hand. They would need it to escape; they would have to have it... and then a coldness shot through him! He realized that the web was not long enough! It would not reach the net! Instead, the little man would be snapped up short, swung back into the flames....

At the last possible moment, Wentworth whipped his hand free of the silk, and it left his hand like the snapped line of a kite. The little man sailed through the air, folded neatly to land in the center of the net. The silken web whipped after him, settled its soft skein about him. On the roof, Ram Singh turned slowly toward Wentworth and there was a grin on his face.

He started to speak, and there was a crashing roar behind

them, a volley of upward flying sparks. The top floor had fallen, and the roof was already curling the soles of their shoes!

"*Wah*, master," cried Ram Singh, "we are trapped like dead Parsees atop a Tower of Silence. But no vultures will ever pick our bones!"

Wentworth's eyes were questing about. If he had the web, there was that roof fifty feet away. But he did not have the web....

"There are vultures below, Ram Singh," he said quietly. "They wear blue coats...."

Ram Singh spat into the flames. "*Wah*, there are no more than two score of them, and we are mighty warriors, thou and I!" He heaved a deep sigh, and coughed violently with the heat. "I should have liked another battle or two!"

Ram Singh threw back his head and bellowed with sudden laughter. "Ha, surely it is a great joke the One True God plays upon us!" he roared. "Now, we have earned the right to live again—and there is no way at all in which to live. *Ah, hoo!* How the One True God can jest!"

CHAPTER 6
STREET SCENE
OF THE DAMNED

IN THE streets about the blazing apartment building, police fought to hold back the hysterical crowds. A thin line of the rescued still filtered down from the adjoining roof, from the court to the rear—but they were those who long ago had been thrust to safety by the Spider. No one could live now in that blazing inferno!

A long block from the apartment, the heat reddened the faces of the struggling police; people held hands before their eyes and even then the blast-furnace temperature struck like a hammer. Beyond the roped-off line, the firemen crouched behind shields to play their hoses. The hundred-pound pressure in the lines hissed and roared from the nozzles but the white gush of the waters seemed not to touch the flames at all. The roar of the roiling flames that bubbled from the windows; the black immensity of the tower of smoke blotted out every other conscious thought. Men stood in stupefied awe of the thing that man had created—and destroyed!

Even the police, bracing their shoulders backward against the crowd, could stare nowhere except at that black smear that was the roof. It had not crashed yet. Every other floor had fallen, but for the moment the roof still held.

"The man's done for," Sergeant O'Leary lifted his hoarse voice above the fire roar, above the murmurous thunder of the crowd behind him. "Not even the Spider could live through that!"

"A great pity," Officer McDonald yelled back at him. "A great pity the fire had to take him… when every man here is straining to line that crook up between his pistol sights!"

Officer McDonald's uniform cap was suddenly snatched from his head and a woman's hands fastened in his hair!

"A pity is it, you dumb flatfoot!" the woman screeched. "A pity is it? The Spider has saved a hundred lives this night and you talking about your guns! You worthless, no good, dumb…."

O'Leary cut in heavily, "All right, there now, mother!" he cried. "Lay off or I'll run you in. Sure, the boy is young yet!"

McDonald ducked away from those vengeful hands, caught up his uniformed cap. His face was hot with something more than the heat, "He's a crook!" McDonald yelled. "I'm telling you...."

"Easy, McDonald!" O'Leary said sternly. "Like I said, you're young, and..." He broke off, cocking an ear as a siren wailed beyond the thick crowd. He burst out strongly. "Make way there! Make way! It's the commissioner himself! I'd know the commissioner's car anywhere, and the way that lad Cassidy plays the siren. Make way! Make way!"

McDonald thrust violently into the crowd, using his strong young back and his shoulders. The woman slapped him as he went past, glowered after him... and O'Leary grinned dourly. The commissioner was on the spot, surely. He was taking no chances where the Spider was concerned!

The crowd parted reluctantly and a car jounced and rocked over the hoses. Leaning from the window, Kirkpatrick's face showed stern and strained in the fierce red glow. He jerked open the door and strode ahead as the car rolled to a final halt beyond the fire-line.

"Has he been seen recently, Sergeant O'Leary?" Kirkpatrick asked crisply.

O'Leary flushed at being recognized by the chief, but Kirkpatrick was always that way. Among eighteen thousand police who worked and fought under him, there were few he could not

call by name—not as a trick to gain their loyalty but because he loved his men....

"That he hasn't, Commissioner," O'Leary growled. "A shadow itself couldn't squeeze through our lines. All the people who escaped are being held apart so he can't pass off as one of them, but..." He stared up where the roof was a faint black smear amid the boiling greedy tongues of flame. "Sure, the devil himself couldn't live there now!"

Kirkpatrick's harried eyes lifted to that high roof and his mouth stretched into a harsh line. "No," he said, and his voice was less crisp than usual. There was pain in his tones. "No, no man could live through that!"

Even as he spoke, there was a rending crash within the building. Fresh gouts of flame gushed through the windows, and sparks flew upward like a swarm of golden birds. The roof had fallen!

KIRKPATRICK WHIPPED toward O'Leary. "Sergeant, take a squad of picked men and work this crowd, fast! Pick up every character known to headquarters, or any other suspicious persons. Bring them here. If the Spider has confederates, this is the time to get them!"

Sergeant O'Leary saluted and spun into the crowd, shouting for men. Sure, the commissioner never forgot anything! And he was remembering now that Sergeant O'Leary had an eye for faces. Let him set his eyes on a crook and he never forgot him! O'Leary's eyes stabbed at the faces about him, and there was an aggressive happiness in his movements... Ah, but it was bad luck the Spider had met this night!

Standing rigidly beside his car, Kirkpatrick could not tear

his eyes away from the joyous leaping of the flames. Dick Wentworth was in there, but he had not been trapped by the flames alone. Nothing so simple as a fire could trap him. The end had come as Kirkpatrick had always known it must; trapped through his great heart, helping people to the last… He shuddered a little, and his jaw's line stood out whitely.

"A hell of a way to die," he muttered.

"Was you speaking, Commissioner?"

Cassidy piped from the driver's seat. "Sure, and ain't that a grand fire?"

Kirkpatrick's voice ripped out sternly. "Keep your ear on that radio, Cassidy! And speak when you're spoken to!"

Cassidy turned his pale hurt eyes on the commissioner's face, and Kirkpatrick swung away. Cassidy fumbled with the radio dials. Something was working on the commissioner, surely.…

Kirkpatrick's eyes whipped toward an ambulance, parked inside the lines. He saw a woman, with a half-completed bandage flying from her arm. She broke away and ran toward him, and there were tears streaming down her face!

"Do something!" she screamed. "Why, don't you *do* something!" She reached Kirkpatrick and her frail fists beat on his chest. Her face was ravaged, and her hair streamed wildly. "For God's sake, Commissioner, the Spider's in there. The Spider.…"

Kirkpatrick's face did not change, but his hands were gentle as he set the woman back. "Easy," he said gently. "There's nothing anyone.…"

"*He* did something!" the woman cried. "He saved my life!

Mine and my man's and my baby's! He saved hundreds… and you stand here and let him die!"

A policeman ran up, took her by the arm roughly. "Sorry, Commissioner!" he panted. "She broke through! Come on, you!"

The woman twisted in the cop's grasp. "Cowards!" she screamed. "All of you cowards! Letting a man die that way! Damn you, oh, damn you—*you want him to die!*"

"Take her away!" Kirkpatrick snapped. "And look to your duty, man!" He turned away, and for a moment his stern face was twisted awry… He was glad when O'Leary came proudly forward, shepherding a dozen stumbling sullen men.

"Come on, there!" O'Leary growled. "Pick it up, you punks. It's the commissioner himself will be looking you over!"

Kirkpatrick stepped up on the running-board of his car to see them better, and his experienced eye leaped over their faces. Small fry, all of them, except….

"Book that man, O'Leary!" Kirkpatrick snapped. "Dapper, you were ordered to stay out of New York! You'll get a year this time!"

O'Leary thrust the man into the waiting hands of a patrolman and Kirkpatrick's eyes raced on. "The rest can go… Hold on there. Jackson! Jackson, come here!"

Kirkpatrick's voice rasped and a broad-shouldered man with a strongly-muscled jaw moved toward him rigidly, like a man lost in thoughts far away. His face was expressionless, but there was suffering in his eyes.

"Where's Wentworth?" Kirkpatrick demanded harshly.

Jackson was a soldier on parade, "At home, sir, I believe. He dismissed me for the night a couple of hours ago."

Kirkpatrick snapped, "You're lying, Jackson! Wentworth never dismisses you when he's working on a case."

Jackson's cheeks burned dully. His back stiffened, "If I'm a liar, sir, then there's no need asking more questions, is it?" He turned his back and started to march away. O'Leary stepped into his path belligerently, but Kirkpatrick motioned him aside.

"Come back, Jackson," he called. "I apologize. Not for calling you a liar, which God knows you are… but for trying to make you talk. But you stay here with me, my man, or I'll run you in. Understand? If Wentworth is counting on your help, he won't get it!"

Jackson's tortured eyes quested toward the building, and Kirkpatrick swore as his own fascinated gaze swung back that way. The flames were yielding finally to the hammer of the water, dying a little.

"All right, O'Leary," Kirkpatrick said quietly. "Good work. Get back to your posts."

Behind Kirkpatrick, Cassidy's shrill voice popped out. "Hey, Commissioner! Hey… *The Spider's on the air!*"

Kirkpatrick whipped about with a violent oath. Jackson restrained a shout that gushed to his throat. He stared toward the flushed face of Kirkpatrick's driver.

"Says he'll give you thirty seconds to get to the car, Commissioner!" Cassidy was babbling. "He's got something to tell you over the radio!"

Kirkpatrick's face was curiously twisted with relief, with

anger, with incredulity. He said, sharply, "Cassidy, you're hearing things! You...."

Cassidy twisted a dial, and a voice leaped suddenly from the radio, loud and full, mocking, curiously vibrant despite its metallic, flat tones.

"Greetings, Commissioner Kirkpatrick! *This is the Spider speaking!*"

KIRKPATRICK'S HANDS set on the side of his car, and the knuckles glistened white as bone. Rigidity crept across his face. Behind him, Jackson let a fleeting smile touch his mouth. He closed his eyes for a moment, and something squeezed from under the corner of the lid, laid a crystal line across his rough, weathered cheek. He brushed at it with a sleeve, and his face went expressionless again. Couldn't fool him on that voice! He'd know it among a million. He was a fool to think the Major could be taken in any such thing as a fire! The Major? Phooey! The Major could walk through hell and come up smiling!

"Here's the message, Kirkpatrick," the Spider's voice went on easily. "The fire you are witnessing—and hoping had done for me—is the work of an arson ring! There will be more such fires unless your valiant officers learn to use their heads better than they use their guns! I can give you only a little help at this time, Kirkpatrick. Things have been a bit too hot even for me!"

Kirkpatrick twisted his head about. "O'Leary! Get direction loops tuned on this message. See if you can locate the source!"

O'Leary bounded toward the fire-lines, but the news had raced before him. In the way of crowds, someone had been listening to that radio; someone had heard the name of the

Spider! There was laughter and shouting beyond the police lines. Cops' uniform caps were suddenly sailing through the air and O'Leary, trying to break through those jumbled ranks, was tossed back like a boy trying to crash a varsity football line!

"Yea! Spider!" a man yelled thinly. "The Spider's alive!"

A hoarse and formless cheer lifted from the crowd. Beside the ambulance, a woman dropped to her knees and her head was bowed. In her arms, she clasped her children and beside her stood a man. He lifted his face, and the red lights from the dying fire played across it, found two glistening streaks that coursed their way from his eye corners downward over his cheeks.

Kirkpatrick was aware of these things in the back of his mind, but his attention was riveted on the radio, and the Spider was still speaking:

"The arson ring operates as a fire insurance company, Kirkpatrick. The lads tried to stop me in the burning building and I had to… remove a few. I'll send you a Spider seal by mail as a memento. On one of them, I found a fire insurance policy. It seems normal, but, listen Kirkpatrick, it guarantees not to repay damages from fires. *It guarantees that there will be no fires!*

"Off-hand, Kirkpatrick, I should call it a protection racket!"

A tall man in a silk hat and formal overcoat made his casual way through the crowd, smiling at its jubilation. There was no sternness on his face, nothing threatening… but he moved easily through the ranks that had hurled the police backward! Men glanced up at his touch on their shoulder, anger, jubilation, hysteria on their faces. They looked into his calming smiling eyes… and somehow, they made way for him, though he only murmured politely, "If you don't mind!"

He stood presently beside Jackson, and the Spider's voice still ran on with its undertone of mockery.

"This organization, Kirkpatrick," it said, "maintains a corps of fire inspection men clothed in white. I am convinced, Kirkpatrick, that these men actually make the racket collections. And the name of this fire insurance company, Kirkpatrick… are you listening…."

The man touched Kirkpatrick on the shoulder with his cane. "I really don't think, Kirk," he said easily, "that the Spider has much to contribute!"

Kirkpatrick whipped about at the echo of that voice. "Dick!" he cried. "Dick Wentworth. Why…" He twisted back toward the radio, from which the Spider's moving voice still sounded. "Dick…."

"The Spider signing off. Kirkpatrick!" came the final words over the air. "When you need me, Kirk, don't bother to look for me… *I'll be there!*"

There was a dying hum, and the voice was gone, but Kirkpatrick turned stiffly toward Wentworth and slowly his hand came up to knuckle the waxed ends of his mustaches, as always when he was puzzled or worried. He shook his head.

WENTWORTH WAS leaning on his cane, smiling easily, "A very minor contribution," Wentworth said dryly.

"The Spider has only told you that the arson ring expects to profit through fires. Anyone could deduce a fire insurance company…."

Cassidy thrust out his carroty head. His hair stood up rigidly as wires upon his pink scalp. "The Spider is a right guy!" he said strenuously. "And he gave us the name of the company, too. The No-More-Fires, Inc. He said it while you was talking!"

"That will do, Cassidy," Kirkpatrick said crisply, but a smile lingered on his mouth. "Not too bright," he muttered to Wentworth, "but I've never had a better driver! Wentworth... Damn it, man, I'm glad to see you!" He thrust out his hand.

Wentworth's tip-tilted brows were mocking below the line of his hat-brim. He accepted Kirkpatrick's handclasp, negligently. "Why, that's kind of you, Kirk," he murmured, "but really, it's only been an hour or so since we met at the Hesperides Club. Or don't you remember?"

Kirkpatrick frowned, but let it pass. "Go along with me, Dick," he said. "I'm going to check up on that arson ring right now!"

Wentworth tapped a yawn, "Surely, No-More-Fires will wait until morning, Kirk," he said. "I confess to a touch of weariness. Afraid I'll have to beg off. Going home now, Jackson?"

Jackson faced Kirkpatrick, "Would there be anything else, sir?" he asked, and there was laughter in his eyes.

Kirkpatrick shook his head, and bewilderment was still in his eyes as he watched the crowd part once more to allow Wentworth to pass through. It occurred to him suddenly that he had not asked Wentworth how he happened to be near the scene of the fire, but... Kirkpatrick shrugged. It would accomplish nothing. If Wentworth were the Spider... But how in the devil could he be? The Spider had been speaking when Wentworth arrived!

Cassidy said truculently, "Imagine that lily-fingered guy throwing off on the Spider! What's *he* ever done...."

"That will do, Cassidy!" Kirkpatrick said sternly. "Speak when you're spoken to. Find O'Leary. Tell him I'll need a squad of men. And find out the address of this No-More-Fires, Inc.!"

Sergeant Reams, who was Kirkpatrick's bodyguard, came running breathlessly. "I tried to get through to you, sir," he cried. "That mob out there... Commissioner, the Spider was just on the air! He got clear!"

Kirkpatrick glared at Sergeant Reams.

"It's the truth, Commissioner, so help me!" Reams blurted.

Kirkpatrick said dryly, "Are you sure, Reams, that it wasn't little Sir Echo you heard?"

He snorted and climbed into the car. Reams took off his uniform cap and scratched his head. He went toward the car. "No, now, listen, Commissioner, I'd be willing to swear...."

IN THE crowd beyond the fire line, Wentworth's stride stretched out and Jackson swung up alongside of him. Their heels clicked on the pavement in regular rhythm, marching men together.

"You're going to that office, too, Major?" Jackson asked quietly. "Too bad Cassidy got the name."

Wentworth smiled. Jackson had got what Kirkpatrick had missed—that Wentworth had tried to keep him from hearing that name, No-More-Fires, Inc. "Quite right," he acknowledged, "I wanted the... enemy to hear that warning, but I didn't want Cassidy's pals on the scene too soon. We'll have to hurry!"

The last of the crowd was behind. Wentworth swiftly led the

way around a corner. Jackson stretched his legs to keep pace. His lips were compressed and his eyes kept reaching up to the face of the man he served.

"In God's name, Major, how did you manage it?"

"The broadcast?" Wentworth asked absently. His mind was racing ahead to the work before him. The police would leave promptly, and he must reach those offices first.

"No, I know about the broadcast," Jackson said quickly. "You recorded the speech on one of those telephone gadgets that uses a wire for a record. But the fire, sir!"

"Oh, that," Wentworth said, his gaze still reaching ahead. "There were plenty of radio aerials to twist into a cable, a roof fifty feet away with a convenient chimney. Simply lassoed it...." He rubbed a gloved palm gingerly. "I can think of more pleasant methods, however, than going hand over hand along such wires as those!"

Jackson spotted the coupé ahead—a coupé to which they all carried duplicate keys, and he leaped ahead to snap open the door. He started, *"Ram Singh!* What the devil! You were on duty guarding Miss Nita!"

Ram Singh glowered at him, *"Wah,* do I take orders from such as thee!"

"Quiet!" Wentworth snapped. "Have you cleared that record off, Ram Singh? Kirkpatrick may follow!"

"Even as commanded, master." Ram Singh's voice was a growl, and his eyes were on Jackson. "It has been drawn through the magnet and is innocent of thy voice!"

"Jackson, take the wheel!" Wentworth snapped.

Jackson swung around the car, and the three crowded into the coupé, which made a swift circuit of the fire area and bore southward at Wentworth's orders. Jackson drove at furious speed, but his eyes strayed now and again to Ram Singh's face.

"There's a knot behind your ear, you dumb heathen!" he ripped out at Ram Singh. "They took you!... Good God, Major, they haven't got... *Miss Nita!*"

Wentworth's tightening lips were sufficient answer, but he told briefly what had happened... how Ram Singh had been called from the car by a voice that had seemed Wentworth's own, and knocked down; the fight in the building. Ram Singh's chest swelled with pride.

"Hadst thou been present," he said stoutly, "thou wouldst have seen two mighty warriors go into battle! Many of the *sahib's* enemies died under my hand!"

Jackson spat out the open window. "Pity you didn't start fighting a little sooner! Miss Nita taken!"

Ram Singh's voice burst out in a roar that showed his pain. "Now by Kali and by Siva, thou jackal...."

"Silence," Wentworth said quietly. "We're on our way now to rescue Miss Nita. Our only chance is through Munro. By putting that Spider message on the air, I warned Munro that the police would be on his trail. If there's anything incriminating in that office, he'll clean it out. We'll find one of his men there. With any luck... Munro himself!"

Ram Singh laughed, *"Wah, sahib!* Let these two hands of mine...."

"Stop at the next corner, Jackson," Wentworth cut in. "Ram

Singh, you will go home. I think there is a good chance that Munro will phone... to threaten about the *missie sahib!* I need a brave man there!"

Ram Singh glowered, "Nay, *sahib*, did I not fight well?"

"Like the warrior you are, my lion," Wentworth said quietly. "There is incense in thy beard!"

Ram Singh's teeth flashed through his beard, as the car stopped. *"Wah*, it is not to battle you go, Jackson!" he said contemptuously. "Were it battle, the master would prefer his warrior!"

Jackson's lips opened, but Wentworth's hand touched his arm, and he said nothing. The car spurted forward, and instantly Wentworth whipped open the compartment which hid his Spider disguise.

"Each man to his own trade, Jackson," he said, "You would not expect a corporal to command a brigade!"

"But Miss Nita, sir!" Jackson's words were a cry. Their loyalty to the brave woman whom Wentworth loved was only less than to their master; second not even to their loyalty to each other. Nita van Sloan could command Jackson and Ram Singh... and these were men who acknowledged few leaders!

Wentworth made no answer. His own heart was sore, and the battle ahead claimed all his concentration. The police would be there quickly. They had no such urgency to drive them as Wentworth's own, but Kirkpatrick would waste no time. The Spider had to get there ahead of the police. He had his own means of making prisoners talk, which the police could not employ. And there might be evidence there which would mean to the Spider the capture of Munro—and the release of Nita!

Jackson said slowly, "You may be walking into a trap, Major. Munro will be expecting… the Spider!"

Working on his disguise, Wentworth did not glance up. He said, quietly, "Of course, Jackson!"

ALONG THE seventh floor corridor of the deserted office building, the man ran swiftly. He checked at a door whose glass was lettered: *No-More-Fires, Inc.* His knuckles played an eccentric tattoo, and the door was whipped open.

The man darted through the darkened outer office toward the inner room where a man with abnormally thick shoulders bent over a mass of papers. The floor was littered; a safe stood open.

"He's here!" the man gasped. "The Spider's here, Daley!"

The man called Daley jerked up his head. His black eyes stabbed into the face of the other, and they were ruthless, sharp eyes, contrasting strangely with the dapper dignity of his gray hair and mustache, his tailored business suit.

"You saw what?" he demanded harshly.

"At the service door," the man panted. "A coupé slowed down there and… and a sort of shadow crossed the sidewalk!"

Daley's dark eyes widened. He nodded briskly. "All right, you five take your stations. Strike a match at the window first, so the boys on the roof will be ready. Remember, do nothing until I give the signal! I don't want to get burned down like Mugsy Lugan!"

The man nodded, swallowed thickly. "The way that Spider gets out of traps…."

Daley said, quietly, "Shut up, Haskins!"

Haskins flinched, ducked his head. "Okay. Okay," he muttered. "You're the boss, but I wish Munro was here."

Daley bent over the papers without more words. He began thrusting some of them back into the safe, tucking others into an inside pocket. They made the breast of his coat bulge a little, and he frowned at that. The office was completely quiet, the men hidden in the huddled darkness of the outer room. He strained his ears and could hear nothing. It did not matter. Everything was ready. His mouth compressed against his teeth. He didn't understand this play of the Spider in using the police....

He turned his back toward the doorway, and slipped aside the blotter on the desk. A ground-glass panel was exposed, and he depressed a button at one corner of the glass. A picture in strong blacks sprang into view in the glass panel, an overhead view of the outer office brought here by an infra-red light relay and television!

He could see what would be hidden in the darkness out there, could see the five men crouched out of sight behind chairs and the divan forming a semi-circle whose center was the door of the inner office. That was how he wanted it. The Spider must be allowed to enter. The difficulty would come when he tried to get out! For a moment, Daley frowned. He hoped the police wouldn't come too soon! But hell, a couple of fire-bombs would block them out, and they had their guns... Daley shrugged, and kept his eye on the panel. Abruptly, he stiffened and bent sharply forward over the panel!

Now....

The outside door of the office had opened... and a shadow

stole inside! A shadow that was a man all in black, shielded by a long black cape that made the outlines of his body amorphous and somehow more menacing than a human shape would have been. Daley stared with slowly widening eyes while that figure poised inside the door. He saw the slow movement of the head as the man looked about him. The man… Good God, he was gazing on the Spider!

DALEY'S HAND shook as he slapped the blotter back into place over the ground-glass panel. Leaning forward across the desk, he snatched up the telephone and dialed a number. The clicking of the mechanism seemed ridiculously loud. Daley was aware of the smallness of the office. Despite the dwindled heat of the building, it seemed very hot in here. A finger slipped under his collar, loosened it a little about his neck.

"Sprague?" he spoke into the phone, and cleared his throat of hoarseness, "Sprague, Daley speaking. Orders from Munro! The Spider has set the police on our trail… No, not yet! They're likely to raid at any minute. Listen, Sprague… Munro wants a meeting of all sub-heads in one hour! Sudden? Yes… Well, maybe you want to argue with Munro! Yes, I thought you'd see it that way. Munro says it's up to you to get the boys together in one hour at the room at the Man o'War. And Munro is getting leery of spies. Here's the password, and give it only to those who are called to the meeting. Ready? All right—*'From my ashes, I arise again!'* That's all, but see every one of the lieutenants is there!"

He slapped up the receiver, and behind him a voice spoke mockingly, "I'm afraid," it said softly, "that one lieutenant will be… indisposed!"

Daley had been expecting something, of course, but he started violently. He whipped about, and his hands clawed at the side of the desk. His cheeks quivered. He touched a tongue to his dry lips. Just inside the door, stood the hunched and sinister figure of the Spider! From beneath the broad brim of the black hat, gray-blue eyes regarded him coldly, unwaveringly. Daley shivered, and the stiffness went out of him.

He said, incredulously, quaveringly. "The... the Spider!"

The figure did not move. "I see that you have saved me a lot of time," the Spider said softly. "I'll take the papers from your inside pocket. But be sure that you bring out only the papers, Daley!" The gun in the Spider's left hand moved slowly, a cold eye, but not more deadly than the gray-blue eyes of the Spider. It lifted, and centered on Daley's forehead!

Daley's hand moved jerkily across his breast, and drew out the papers Wentworth had indicated—and only the papers. His black eyes wavered away from the Spider's and fell.

"Don't... Don't kill me, Spider!" he whispered.

Wentworth laughed, and the sound was mocking, more menacing than any words. "Why, not yet, Daley," he said. "Perhaps, not at all! It will depend on you, Daley. On how much you know! You will notice, Daley, that I do not say how much you will tell... We know that, Daley." He was moving softly forward. His cape made his advance a silken, ominous glide. "Yes, indeed, we know that. You will tell everything, Daley! *Turn around!*"

Daley stiffened, turned on wooden feet. His hands were yanked down behind him, and rope bit into his flesh. He did not struggle at all. He was thrust into the chair behind the desk. His eyes followed the crisp movements of the Spider, the sure speed with which his gloved hands shuffled through the papers of the safe. Daley licked his lips. This was not going exactly as he had planned. This was the time when he should break for it, throw himself into the outer office and call on the others to shoot down the Spider. This was the time… Daley sat very still.

A thin distant wail sliced into the room and Daley stiffened. The Spider had not moved from his swift contemplation of the papers, but he spoke casually. "Ah, yes, the police," he murmured, "but don't worry, Daley. They won't get here in time to help… or hurt you!" He seemed to move almost idly, and yet the Spider was across the room in a bound, had yanked Daley from the chair and thrown his weight across his shoulder.

"We still have a little time, Daley," he said gently, "and I have further business. It may seem a shame to you to spoil this fine office, but I think a spot of fire here would be a good idea. You guarantee your clients will not have fires, don't you, Daley? Don't you think it may make your path more difficult… if your office is destroyed by fire?"

Carelessly Wentworth tossed Daley into the outer office! HE SPRANG back beside the desk then, and his hands moved swiftly. He whipped out several glass containers from beneath his cloak and smashed them against the walls. The reek of benzine struck across the office. Wentworth swept the papers from the desk, brought out his lighter… and paused, rigidly. He had swept aside the blotter, and he was staring down at the ground-glass panel!

Instantly, his keen mind leaped to the use of the panel. His hand flicked to the button and depressed it, and he gazed down at the infra-red view of the outer office. Daley, already freed, was being led across the office toward a place of concealment. As Wentworth watched, Daley's hands lifted, and he stripped off the wig… His whole face seemed to come off with the touch of his hands!

In still amazement, Wentworth watched. There had been terror in the crouch of those ambushers a moment ago, but now suddenly there was confidence in their poise. The guns lifted bravely in their hands. And Wentworth knew why! Daley had stripped off a disguise. Daley was… *Munro!*

Wentworth's lips twisted in a slow smile, and the expression of his face was ominous! He laid his guns on the desk before him, and his eyes quested over the thin partition of glass and wood that separated him from the outer room, shifted back to the view in the panel—and a curse leaped to his lips. Munro had faced toward him now, and for the first time he saw the man's face. He saw where a face *should* be. God! The man… *The man had no face!*

The flesh was welted and corded across his countenance as if by a horrible burn. The mouth was a twisted, gaping smear, and the eyes were red-rimmed, drawn to awful slits! If this was the face of Munro… Wentworth cut off his thoughts. The police sirens were shrieking to crescendo. In a few moments' time, they would be crashing into the building, and he had a score to settle first!

Wentworth looked down again at the ground-glass panel, looked toward the walls and deliberately lifted his two guns.

He could not be absolutely sure of his first shot through those obstacles, but with the aid of the ground-glass panel he could soon get the range!

Wentworth thrust out his two automatics at arm's-length, a thing the Spider rarely found necessary to do. Eyes on the panel, he squeezed the two triggers together!

The crash of the guns in the office was thunderous. The wooden partition of the wall held two torn and splintered holes... and in the infra-red panel, Wentworth saw the glass of the outer door crash to the floor! But Munro... Munro who had stood there a moment before, was flat on the floor behind a desk! The other men were on their feet, and their guns began to speak!

Wentworth smiled bitterly. Munro was for the moment beyond his reach, but when he arose again, the guns of the Spider would be more certain! He began to shoot!

At the same instant, he heard the window crash out behind him, and there was a muffled blast on the floor. He saw gouts of liquid flame hurdle past him—and in the same instant, the benzine which he had scattered against the walls caught fire! In a breath, the walls of the room were curtains of flame!

The end....

Outside the office door, the guns of the killers were crashing! Wentworth saw a gun spurt upward from the spot where Munro lay, and suddenly the infra-red panel went blank! And the sirens of the police had wailed to a finish out in the streets.

Trapped... Doubly trapped by flames and the guns of these

men outside, his advantage of the infra-red panel destroyed. And the police were outside. Wentworth lifted his two automatics, crouched in the shelter of the desk. Wentworth lifted the guns… and then the Spider laughed aloud!

CHAPTER 7
MURDER CONFERENCE

I N THAT outer office, men heard the laughter of the Spider and clutched their guns more fiercely. The bright red glare of the flames lifted behind the partition, threw its light out through the ground glass of the door.

"Wait!" Munro's voice said harshly. "He can't see you now, and he'll have to come out. And don't worry about the police. I'll blast a way through them!"

Abruptly, the door of the inner office whipped open. The caped, hunched outline of the Spider glided smoothly forward, and guns reached out their red lances from its sides. With a hysterical fury, the guns of the gangsters answered! They cursed and shouted in the release of their tension, hurled lead with both hands. The figure of the Spider had stopped, and there were no more shots from him.

"I got him, Frenchy!" a hoarse voice shouted. "I got three bullets in him!"

"I got five!" Frenchy yelled back.

The guns, emptied once, began to hammer again… and still there was no answering fire. And yet, suddenly, the Spider laughed!

The eerie sound of that mocking mirth mounted above the fury of the guns, above the crackling roar of the fire within the inner office. It stopped the shooting; it cut off the voices of men. Then, with a shriek of pure terror, one man bolted out through the doorway. Another followed.

"You can't kill him!" he shrieked. "Oh, God, you can't kill him!"

That whole office was full of sudden panic, and men fighting to escape. From a remote corner of the office, a figure lifted—minus hat and cape—and the two guns in his fists rolled rhythmically. Three men went down in that huddle at the doorway, but the others escaped. Wentworth reached them in two long leaps, whipped them over on their backs—and swore raspingly. The Faceless One, Munro, was not among them!

Fiercely, Wentworth sprang toward where the figure of the Spider apparently stood. He yanked cape and hat and flung them about his own body, sprang for the door with the cape kiting from his shoulders. Where the Spider apparently had stood, there was revealed a tall desk lamp standing upon a swivel, roller-bearing chair. In their hysterical fear, the killers had mistaken that draped chair, with Wentworth prone behind to push it forward, to fire his guns that one time, for the figure of the Spider!

Beside the outer door, Wentworth paused for a single moment. He stooped, and his cigarette-lighter glinted in his hand... and when he sped on along the hallway, he left a glistening challenge for Munro, a mockery for the police who at least would not have to solve this crime... The Spider had stamped his signature upon his kill—*the seal of the Spider!*

But Wentworth ran with fury in his blood. Once more, he had been face to face with Munro, and the man had slipped between his fingers! He recalled that flame-seared countenance and something like a shudder traced its way up Wentworth's spine. If that was the face of Munro, it was no wonder the man had become a genius at disguise!

The battle was not yet lost. The police would be on guard below, warned by the crash of shots and the lurid glare of the flames! If he could contrive to throw Munro into their hands....

Wentworth raced down the fire-escape stairs by which he had ascended, and suddenly heard the crackle of shots

Guns reached out their red lances at the hunched figure of the Spider!

below, and a muffled detonation that was followed by the mad screams of men in awful pain! He swerved out into the first-floor corridor, and saw… *hell!* Three policemen were down, motionless in death, and two others ran crazily for the exit with flame streaming from their garments! Even as Wentworth saw them, their companions reached for the men and hurled them to the ground to extinguish the fires—and Wentworth heard Kirkpatrick's sharply crisp voice rap out, organizing pursuit!

Wentworth ducked back into the stairway, raced quietly for the service entrance which his lockpick had opened for him a little earlier. He could do no more out there than the police were accomplishing, for Munro had once more made good his escape! But there was something he still could do… He could attend the meeting of Munro's associates. He knew the place, the time, and the password!

His black-caped figure merged with the shadows against the building, to appear presently beside the parked coupé where Jackson waited feverishly. The car leaped forward under Jackson's instant touch, sped northward.

"You called Ram Singh?" Wentworth asked sharply.

Jackson nodded curtly. "No word, sir."

Wentworth knotted his fists on his knees. "Munro is still ahead of me," he said swiftly. "He was waiting for me back there… and he has set another trap for me. Know where the Man o' War is?"

"A tough dive on the waterfront, sir," Jackson nodded. "What do you mean—a trap?"

Wentworth smiled faintly. "Munro was in that office. He saw

me come in, by means of a television rig-up. Then he picked up a phone and gave me the information as to when, where, and how to enter a meeting he was calling! That was in case his trap there did not succeed in catching me."

Jackson said frantically, "For God's sake, Major, must you go? That place will be alive with his killers! He'll be expecting you! Must you really go?"

Wentworth's head swung toward him, and there was surprise in his eyes. "Munro will be there," he said quietly.

THE ROOM above the Man o' War was reserved for the initiated. It was crowded now by more than twenty men who sat around wet tables and tossed their drinks. Their faces were a rogue's gallery of the unconvicted murder-men of the country's mobs. At the door, an emaciated man with a caved-in chest, a knife gash purple on one cheek, kept watch. It was to him the men whispered one by one, "From my ashes, I arise again!"

His voice was a whisper, but it was a whisper from which men shrank. There was a sardonic gleam in the man's eyes, and once when he turned quickly, the skirt of his coat lifted to show the sheath of a long-bladed knife. He was the guard, the auditor.

In a corner where little light shone, Sprague sat with both elbows spread on the table. He had a reddened, belligerent face, and his fists were knotted.

"One hour, I get to haul all the boys in," he rumbled. "Hell of a note!"

"Pipe down, Sprague," one of his companions whispered. He twisted his wry neck about, made a snuffling noise in his nose.

"Geez, you don't never know where Munro is going to turn up, or what he'll look like." His snuffling was like weeping. "Geez!"

"That's all right for you, Sniffer," Sprague growled. "Me, I'm responsible, and I wouldn't want to have to make no excuses to Munro!"

The third man at the table moved his thin lips in a smile, and lifted his glass daintily. "I never saw the lad at the next table before—the one with the glass eye. That might be Munro!"

Sprague wrenched about in his chair. "Where, Duke?" he whispered. Sniffer made faint worried sounds in his nose.

"Oh, him!" Sprague frowned. "Naw, I ain't never seen him before. It might be Munro... and then again... *it might be the Spider!*"

Duke set his glass down so suddenly, liquor slopped on his hand, and he did not bother to wipe it off. "My God!" he said. "So that's what we're here for!"

Sniffer pushed his chair back. "Look, Sprague," he snuffled. "You don't want me here. You don't..." The man at the next table looked toward him casually, and Sniffer slumped back in his chair. Sprague watched sardonically, and Duke was using a silk handkerchief on his liquor-wet hand, frowning.

Sprague said, "The Chief arranged things so the Spider would be here. The Chief will be here, too. If we spot the Spider, we burn him down without waiting for orders. If we don't... the Chief will point him out."

Sniffer whined, "I don't like this business of not knowing who the guy next to you is! Geez, for all we know...."

"Whiskey or beer?" a voice rasped at his elbow, and Sniffer

jerked in his chair. He snuffled plaintively as he looked up into the bored face of a waiter.

"Whiskey, damn you, and quit creeping up on a guy!"

The waiter swabbed the table. "Knifer says everybody's already here, Sprague. You're to start the ball rolling!"

Sprague grunted, "Me!"

The waiter smiled and walked carelessly away. He had the slouching stride of a waiter, and the bored look. He didn't look at anybody, and he saw everything. He saw Knifer with his narrow shoulders braced against the door, that thin smile perpetually on his face from the tear of the knife-gash across his cheek. He saw the tautness everywhere, and he knew the whisper had gone the rounds. The Spider was coming… Munro was coming. And nobody knew how either one would appear.

The waiter smiled slightly, and filled three more glasses with whisky. From his sleeve, a thin film of a whitish powder sifted into each glass. He slapped them down on Sprague's table, just as the man reared to his feet.

He beat on the table with his big fist. "All right," he growled, "It's lucky you mugs all got here on time. The Chief ain't taking no foolishness. The Spider has been acting up!"

There had been a noisy, half-apprehensive gabble a few moments before, but it died under Sprague's words. They sat stiffly at their tables, and their necks turned slowly, rigidly. They looked out of their eye corners at their neighbors. In the silence, the waiter moved carelessly away across the room. It was fortunate that the coat he had taken from the regular waiter of the

Man o'War fitted him loosely. That way, the twin guns beneath his arms did not show!

SPRAGUE WAS still growling out words, but Wentworth—the waiter—was paying little heed to them. He had been here for half an hour and still he had not spotted Munro. It might be anyone of them, from Knifer or Sprague to the man behind the bar.

"We got a little job to do," Sprague was saying, "Tonight, the Spider caused us plenty of grief. He turned the police on our tail, and we got to get our customers in line to see that none of them talks. Duke, you and Frosty will take the job. I'll give you the names. Come over here, Frosty! It's a simple business. We're just going to burn a couple of guys alive. After that, there won't be nobody to talk!"

There were loud guffaws from a few of the tables, but the other men waited uneasily. This was just the preamble. The real business of the night would come when the Spider showed himself. The Spider… Their eyes slid about slyly.

The waiter was in a dark corner. It was necessary just now, for there was a terrible anger in his eyes! Burn two men alive… He had to finish his business here quickly and protect those men.

Frosty was swaggering back across the room now from Sprague's table—a white-faced, white-haired killer who had never taken the rap. Wentworth knew him well and, as he looked at the man, his plan was swiftly made! Frosty would have to pass close to him… and with Frosty's help, the Spider would find Munro!

"Hey, Frosty!" he grumbled. "I got a word for you from…."

He let his voice trail off and Frosty swung toward him, unsuspiciously. Wentworth held out the hand over which the wet cloth that he used on the tables was draped. He whipped that towel back, and a gun glinted in the dim light of the corner... and a ring gleamed on Wentworth's finger. It was a ring with a dark stone, but when he pressed on its under-surface as he did now, a red fire glowed in the heart of that stone—a red fire that held the shape of a Spider!

There was naked flame in the eyes of the Spider, too, and they struck against Frosty's.

"Come close to me, Frosty," he said coldly. "If you whisper, you die! Now, into this side room!"

A hard trembling was on Frosty's body, but Wentworth scarcely touched him. His left hand flicked to the under-arm gun, whipped it out. A twist of that hand, and the bullets thudded softly to the floor. He thrust the gun into Frosty's hand.

"Now, Frosty," he said quietly, "we will go back into the dining-room. When we are outside, you will climb on a table, and you will keep that gun in your hand—or you will have a neat little red seal printed on your forehead. Get the picture, Frosty?"

Frosty quavered, "What are you going to do? Geez, Spider, I ain't done nothing yet!"

"No, not yet!" Wentworth told him dryly. "Only three murders that I could be sure of, Frosty. Now... up on that table! Now, yell to make them look at you! Say, 'Hey, you mugs!' Nothing else!"

Frosty climbed fumblingly to the table-top, and a few startled eyes whipped his way. The gun was in his fist. He opened his lips to shout, but it was Wentworth's voice that carried across the room from where he crouched in the shadows….

"Munro!" came the Spider's flat, challenging voice. "Munro! I have come for you! *The Spider has come for you!*"

Chairs slammed backward, tables were pitched forward to the floor while men flung themselves behind those barricades! In the same instant, their guns began to speak! They roared to a swift climax of fury. Lead hammered into Frosty's twitching body.

But unseen in the shadows, Wentworth crouched warily, and his eyes swept the room. His plan was simple enough. Once the Spider was exposed, Munro would have no reason for concealment. He would want to take charge and make sure that the Spider died!

As that first dread challenge of the Spider ripped out, and the deluge of bullets began, Wentworth saw Sprague whip to his feet. But it was not Sprague who shouted out clear orders; who swiftly hurled guards at all the doors, and organized the blockade of the windows so that the Spider should not escape!

It was the trembling man known as Sniffer!

And Sniffer's finger was pointing toward the shadows where the Spider crouched!

"Fools!" Sniffer shouted. "You're killing one of your own friends! There's the Spider… *the waiter who has been serving you drinks!*"

WENTWORTH SPRANG suddenly from the shadows, and about his shoulders was the cape of the Spider, whipped from the darkness of that small room behind him.

His two guns spat together in his fists, and the body of

Sniffer—of Munro!—jerked to the impact. He was picked up and slammed backward over a chair, behind a table!

That was the moment when the lights went out....

In the darkness, a voice rang out clearly while Wentworth crouched low and bounded toward the spot where Munro had fallen. And Wentworth knew that voice. It was the voice of Munro, and it was clear and unshaken with pain!

"Turn on the lights, you damned fools!" it shouted. "The Spider wants it dark! The lights...."

Wentworth flung a bullet questing toward that voice, and near him a man shrieked to the pain of the lead. Somebody had been in the way... Wentworth raced, and in the middle of the floor, he caught a glimpse of a pencil of light as a trapdoor opened. He caught a glimpse of a face that was seared by flame, twisted beyond human recognition—the Faceless One!

Wentworth checked and lifted both guns deliberately... and a chair crashed against his shoulders.

Instantly, Wentworth was on his feet, racing toward the spot where he had seen the trapdoor. There were screams and shouts behind him, and the flicker of crazy gunfire as each man shot at the shadows about him—the shadows that might hold the Spider! Wentworth groped with sensitive hands upon the floor. He found the ridge of the trapdoor, but it was already bolted fast from beneath! He cursed. His two bullets had hit Munro, he knew, but his voice afterward had been clear, and unstrained. Wentworth knew what that meant! Munro had worn a bullet-proof vest!

And now the Faceless One was making good his escape while death swept its dark silent wings through this meeting-room!

Wentworth whirled and went with long leaps toward the door. He needed light to tell him where it was! Overturned tables were in his path, and once he sprawled painfully.

"That you, Duke?" a frightened voice.

"Yeah," Wentworth's tone was the sardonic voice of Duke. "That you, Sprague?"

As he spoke, he leaped… and struck with the barrel of his automatic. There was the crunch of the steel hitting bone, the thud as Sprague's head was driven against the door… and no sound as he fell because Wentworth eased him down softly. A moment later, he wrenched open the door and ducked out.

A bar of light slashed into the darkness and for that instant, the hunched, becaped figure of the Spider was clearly outlined. There was a blasting of guns, a concerted rush for the revealed opening. Wentworth locked the door and flung himself down the stairs, whirled back toward the rear of the *Man o' War* where the trapdoor had opened. He hit a door with his shoulder and it slammed open… and he was gazing into an empty garage, whose doors stood ajar. Overhead, there was a counterbalanced stairway and the locked trapdoor.

This way, Munro had fled… but he was gone past all capture now. And the press of gunmen was hard at Wentworth's heels!

Wentworth did not worry greatly about that pursuit.

Before Munro could get his men together, Wentworth must somehow save the men who were fated to be… burned alive! It did not matter that Wentworth knew the names of the two who were selected. Two more could easily be chosen! There was a hard-riding anger within Wentworth as he flung himself again into the coupé beside Jackson and ordered him harshly northward.

"A telephone, Jackson," he said quietly.

IT WAS Wentworth himself who stepped from the coupé a few minutes later, Wentworth in dark tweeds, with a loose top-coat to shelter him from the sharpness of the winter wind, and neatly gloved hands. He moved swiftly, but more because of the complete efficiency of his every movement rather than because of hurried stride. There was an empty booth in the all-night drugstore which Jackson had chosen, and no one paid any heed to the quiet, self-contained man who slid into that booth. He snapped out the phone number of the district attorney.

Finally a sleepy voice came over the wire, "Wilton Toley speaking! Who is this?"

Wentworth laughed, "The Spider speaking, Toley. Are you awake yet—you who sleep while crime ravages the city!"

Toley stammered, "What... Who? The Spider? Damn your soul...."

Wentworth's voice cut in crisply, "In one hour, Toley, be at your office, and I will turn over to you one of the biggest cases of your career, complete with written evidence and witnesses. The police already are taking in most of the guilty men."

"What is it, man?" snapped Toley. Wentworth eased the receiver onto its hook. He did not need to say more, for Toley knew, as everyone knew, that the word of the Spider was inviolate!

Wentworth reached the coupé in a few swift seconds, long before Toley could get his befuddled senses together and think to trace the call... Wentworth sat easily against the cushions, though he was beginning to feel some of the strain of the long night.

"Jackson," he said quietly, "I have in my pocket a list of the garages where the white fire-trucks of the No-More-Fire Company are kept; also a list of their clients. I think if we borrow one of those white trucks, we will have very little difficulty in persuading the clients to accompany us!"

It was simple to acquire one of the trucks. There was only one man in the garage, for Munro's forces had been heavily depleted by the hours of battling against the Spider. Jackson slipped up and struck him neatly across the temple with a blackjack... Afterward, two men wearing the long white raincoats of the No-More-Fire inspection service, and the red helmets, tooled one of the heavy fire-trucks through the city streets... Wentworth made the first stop at an expensive apartment house, shouldered past the insistent doorman and left Jackson to watch over him. He hammered at a door then until an irritated man of middle age swung it wide. His sleepy eyes started wide, and he flinched back from the door.

"Jeremiah Wilton," said Wentworth in a hard voice, "you will come with me."

"I've paid off," the man stammered. "I paid off for the factory and for my apartment!"

"Come with me!" Wentworth ordered inexorably.

He allowed the man to pull on an overcoat from the hall closet and herded him to the white truck; and they pushed on to the next address. It was a shade over an hour later that the truck was blundering down Lafayette Street through the darkness of early morning. Wentworth had long ago abandoned the driving of the truck to his first captive, Milton; he had dropped Jackson at the last address. Now Wentworth stood at the extreme rear of the truck while Milton drove the last long way to the district attorney's office. Ahead of him were eleven other captives—all clients of No-More-Fires.

Wentworth began to talk quietly, but his voice reached clearly to every man on that truck.

"You think you are the prisoners of the racketeers that have been victimizing you," he said quietly. "You are wrong! You are the prisoners of the Spider!" A moan went up from several of the men. They twisted about, and what they saw was no longer the white fireman with his red helmet. Instead, it was the Spider who stood erect in the rear of the truck. "I will tell you the reason," he went on steadily. "If you obey me, you have nothing to fear! If you refuse... may God have mercy on your souls—for I won't! Gentlemen, we are about to pay a visit to the district attorney. You will tell him everything you know about No-More-Fires!"

"No," a man cried. "Oh, God, they'll kill us all!"

Wentworth said grimly, "It is not a question of that at all! It is merely a question of who kills you! Obey me, or you will find

121

death close upon your heels. Perhaps, you have never seen the seal of the Spider!"

A FEW moments later, Wilton pulled the white truck to a halt before the district attorney's office. Instantly, a horde of police charged from the darkness. Brilliant lights played over the truck, and guns covered every inch of it!

A police lieutenant leaped to the running-board, grabbed Wilton by the collar. "Where's the Spider, you?" he snapped. Wilton struggled in his grasp, twisted toward the rear. "Back there!" he said. "He was back there, and… Good God, the Spider is gone!"

The police searched, but there was no evidence that the Spider had ever been aboard that truck… except that on its sign, there glittered the ominous red seal of the Spider! The police did not know that Wentworth had taken only twelve prisoners; they only noticed that thirteen men walked into the room where District Attorney Toley paced angrily up and down behind his desk. He stopped and glared toward the thirteen men.

"All right!" he snapped. "All right! You've been paying money to racketeers! The police know all about it! I'll take your names, and afterward you'll tell me the whole truth."

Complete silence followed his tirade, but one man, more completely dressed than most of the others, shuffled forward. His hair was pulled down over his forehead, and there was wildness in his straining gray-blue eyes.

"Listen," he said, in a high voice, "you can't do this to me! We're American citizens, and you can't do this to any of us!"

"What's your name?" Toley snapped.

THE SPIDER AND THE FACELESS ONE

The man backed up.

"Look!" he shouted. "Look, the Spider!"

He pointed toward the ceiling, and there, ghostly against the white of the ceiling, but clear despite the lights of the room… there danced the shadow of the Spider! Terror broke the voices of the men, and in the confusion, the laughter of the Spider sounded in the room! Jeremiah Wilton dropped to his knees, "I'll talk. God, yes, I'll talk—only don't let the Spider get me!"

IN THE bedlam over the Spider's laughter, the man who had first challenged Toley slipped from the room into an adjoining office. He ran through a series of connecting rooms then, and as he ran he adjusted his hair, stripped off the slight disguise he had worn.

In a room where Jackson had deposited them earlier, by racing ahead of the white fire-truck after their last capture, he found his quiet tweeds and his topcoat and rapidly donned them. A douse of the acid he carried sufficed to set them fuming. Soon they would be entirely destroyed. He glanced out to make sure that the hallway was empty, and strode toward the front door. He was just opposite the doorway of the hearing room when he saw the familiar crisp-striding figure of Kirkpatrick entering the building!

Wentworth whipped toward the door and beat on it with his fist. He was still hammering, unheard in the bedlam within, when Kirkpatrick strode to his side.

"What are you doing here, Dick?" he asked wearily.

Wentworth whipped toward him. "In God's name, get me inside there, Kirk," he demanded. "There's a white fire-truck outside, and there are No-More-Fire witnesses inside. Kirk, I've got to hear them, got to find out about Munro!"

"He has added two more crimes to his roster, tonight," Kirkpatrick pounded on. "We found two clients of No-More-Fires burned to death!"

Wentworth felt the shock of fear and surprise run through him. He had thought he had found them all, had them safe! Damn Munro! For all he could tell, the fiend had simply picked up any likely victim. Easy enough to make them seem clients of No-More-Fires!

"That makes my news even worse, Kirk," he said heavily. "Nita was kidnapped by Munro!"

Kirkpatrick swore raspingly, and Wentworth gave him the details how Ram Singh had been hit over the head, and Munro had taken his place. Kirkpatrick shuddered.

"The man is uncanny!" he cried. "God alone knows in what disguise he will appear next! Dick, you go home and let me handle this business inside. Toley isn't too fond of you, you know, and I promise that if there is anything definite that will lead to Munro; anything that will help you find Nita, I'll give it to you at once!"

Wentworth let his shoulders sag, "You are right, Kirk," he said. "I was half-crazy. On my way down to see you when I saw that white fire truck, and…."

A door opened across the hall, and a man in police blue thrust out his head. "Mr. Wentworth," he said, "there's a call on this phone for you!"

Wentworth stiffened to a sudden certainty that he knew the

nature of that call! Kirkpatrick was striding beside him as they crossed the corridor, but Wentworth's hand was stone-steady when he caught up the phone.

"Richard Wentworth here," he said.

He saw Kirkpatrick snatching up another phone, putting a tracer on the call, and the voice of Munro was rasping in his ear!

"Done a pretty neat job tonight, haven't you, Wentworth?" said Munro slowly. "Rounded up a lot of clients and forced them to talk, wiped out dozens of my men and thrown them into the hands of the police?"

Wentworth said mockingly, "That's good news, Munro, but I'm afraid you have the wrong party. I understand the Spider has done a few things this night!"

Munro ripped out an oath, and then the cool mockery returned to his voice. "Ah, I see, not you, but the Spider. Under those circumstances, I must change my plans a little. Your Hindu lad told me where to reach you, in case you're interested. But you are interested only in my message, aren't you Wentworth. In... *Nita?*"

Wentworth said coldly, "If you harm her, Munro, you will not survive the night!"

Munro laughed quietly, "Oh, I fancy I will. You will return to your home, Wentworth, and await further instructions from me via telephone. And, oh, yes, you'd better get in touch with your friend, the Spider, in the meantime. You see, Wentworth, I intend to burn Nita alive... unless you can persuade the Spider to put himself on the spot for you!

"Understand, Wentworth?

"Unless you can put the Spider on the spot, at a time and a place I will give you in three hours time… *Nita will be burned alive!*"

CHAPTER 8
HOUR OF SACRIFICE

WENTWORTH HEARD the click of disconnection and whipped toward Kirkpatrick, who was swearing bitterly at delays on the line, unable to get through to a telephone company official. Even while he working, Wentworth knew it was hopeless. Damn it, Ram Singh should have phoned him, and… Wentworth shook his head. Ram Singh had not known where he was. Munro must have seen him entering the building, or a spy reported it. The latter was more likely.

Wentworth weaved a little on his feet as he started toward the door, thrust out a hand to steady himself. Into the room bounced District Attorney Toley.

"I've got one thing to thank the Spider for," he chortled. "The biggest case of my career! Kirkpatrick, I want a complete round-up of that gang within twenty-four hours! I'll hold these men here, shove them into the grand jury first thing in the morning… I'll have indictments by noon. But don't wait for that, Kirkpatrick. Get busy!"

He bounced out of the room again, and Kirkpatrick crossed to Wentworth's side. "It was Munro, wasn't it, threatening Nita?"

Wentworth said, "Yes, he seems to blame me for what the Spider did." His voice was dull.

126

Kirkpatrick's voice was kind. "Go home, Dick, and rest. This is all cleaned up, I tell you! We'll have every man behind the bars in twenty-four hours!"

The laughter that pushed out between Wentworth's grim lips was bitter. "Aren't you forgetting... Munro?" he asked softly.

"We'll find men who will talk!" Kirkpatrick said, but his voice lacked confidence.

Wentworth shook his head. "They will describe to you a man called Munro—a man whose face has been seared and twisted by flame until it is scarcely human, whose eyes are red-rimmed, bleared sockets."

"No man like that can hide long from us!"

"You miss the point, Kirk," Wentworth said quietly. "No man like that could possibly assume the disguise of a normal face." His voice dropped, wearily. "The semblance of the Faceless One is merely another disguise. Good luck in your round-up, Kirk, and if you can find out anything about Nita...."

Kirkpatrick's arm tightened about Wentworth's shoulders. They made a strange picture in that scene of triumph. There was bounce to the stride of the district attorney's aides as they scurried about his business; even the police seemed to have a stiffer, more confident poise. But there was a perceptible droop to Wentworth's shoulders, and Kirkpatrick's face was gouged by lines of anger and frustration. His arm dropped and, slowly, he knuckled his waxed mustaches, as always when he was worried.

"As long as Munro is at large," he said gruffly, "we have gained very little by this round-up. His use of fire is a terrible weapon that he knows too well how to use. He will use it as long as he is at liberty."

"And only the more terribly because of this round-up," Wentworth agreed gravely. "We are chasing phantoms in the dark, and we find only the habiliments of trickery… empty disguises. If I may suggest, Kirk, it would be a good idea to take a talking-picture record of every one of the prisoners, especially watching the sonograph. A man may disguise his voice, but there will be peculiarities there that he himself will not know. The sonograph will show that in sound vibrations!"

Kirkpatrick's eyes narrowed. "You think that Munro is one of those men who are… supposed to be his victims?"

Wentworth lifted his shoulders in a slow shrug. "I do not know. Kirk. It would be clever, in fact the only way he could learn the exact status of the case against him. I have studied each of those men in detail and I can't identify Munro, but I think Munro will call me again about Nita. I will take a sonograph record of the voice… We must catch at straws to identify that man!"

Kirkpatrick said crisply, "I'll do it, Dick! If we can trap a man by the way his voice makes the air vibrate…."

"Then we will have added a page to the science of crime-detection," Wentworth smiled slightly. "I hold out no great hopes, Kirk. It is predicated on the possibility that Munro is in that room. Make sure that Toley keeps them prisoners!" He nodded. "If you want me in the next three hours, Kirk… After that, you can leave any information about Nita with Ram Singh. I'll be… out!"

He strode down the broad corridor, and the eyes of the police followed him respectfully. There was a tangle of newspapermen outside the doors and they yelped eager questions at him. Wentworth shook his head.

"You'll have to see Toley, or Kirkpatrick," he said. "I came on private business."

They followed him to the Daimler, where Jackson waited behind the wheel, and he turned at the door there.

"You may quote me as saying that the Spider has done a great piece of work," he answered their barrage. "I envy him the accomplishment! Will you publish my request that the Spider communicate with me on a matter of vital importance... to me?"

He leaned back against the cushions then and Jackson slapped the door shut, drove swiftly, smoothly back toward Wentworth's apartment. Wentworth fought against the despair that closed in on his heart, and for the first time allowed himself to think deliberately of Munro's demands.

IT WAS like Munro to phrase his demand as he had: that Wentworth must put the Spider on the spot. Munro had no doubts that he and the Spider were the same man, though he had no positive proof of it. Wentworth allowed a faint smile to move his lips. Munro needed no proof. All any criminal needed was a suspicion. Well, he could make certain preparations. Munro had said he would call again in three hours time to tell Wentworth where and when the Spider must be sacrificed.

Somehow, he must contrive to turn that death-trap for the Spider—into a snare that would accomplish Munro's death! Munro was shrewd enough to guess in advance that he would make just such an attempt. So when Munro called, it was a certainty that he would allow Wentworth only the slimmest margin of time… Round and round the cycle of weary thought raced. It had been almost forty-eight hours since he had slept, and his food had been snatched inadequately. Body and brain had been functioning at super-speed, strained to their utmost. He… He was tired. And, dear God, the greatest battle lay ahead: the battle to destroy Munro and save Nita's sweet life.

Wentworth tried to exert his will toward rest, and his mind would not. Munro was not finished; his vanity would not permit him to drop the fight now that his superficial organization had been smashed. Wentworth stiffened at the conviction that this trap for the Spider was only a small part of Munro's plans. He would time it beautifully, and while the Spider was walking into a trap—somewhere in the city, Munro would strike a terrible blow with his weapons of living flame!

His hands knotting to slow, white fists on his knees, Wentworth realized that for the present he was utterly helpless to discover where Munro would strike. He could only guess at the nature of the crime… but he knew how shrewdly and terribly Munro could plan. It was a safe guess that it would entail a wanton slaughter of human beings to cover the final escape!

A crystal-clear chiming of bells broke across Wentworth's thoughts and he lifted his head to stare about him. The dawn was lifting grayly out of the East. There was a bitter, bracing cold in the air against which the few persons abroad moved swiftly, with heads bowed. The doors of a cathedral stood open and men and women were hurrying up the broad, shallow steps.

"This isn't Sunday," Wentworth said dully.

Jackson shook his head, and there was grief and pity on his face as he turned it for an instant while the car slid to a halt at a traffic light.

"No, Major," he said. "Not Sunday. This is Thanksgiving Day."

Wentworth fought down the mockery of the laughter that surged to his lips. Slowly, he forced himself to relax again against the cushions. Thanksgiving Day.

The first hour that Wentworth spent at his home, high above Fifth Avenue where the wind was clean and sharp, was a time of violent activity. He had Jackson rig a recording-machine to take down the words of Munro, and the voice, when he called again. He made arrangements with the telephone company to trace instantaneously any call that came in over his wires. His car was parked at the curb, ready to race at an instant's notice, and he had Ram Singh rent a seaplane and fly it to the nearest pier in the East River, anchor it there.

Afterward, he sent Jackson after more of the flame-extinguishers and to purchase asbestos cloth with which to line the cape of the Spider and fashion a mask. For the moment, it was all he could do; Kirkpatrick would be pressing the questioning of the prisoners, rounding up whatever of Munro's associates could be found… Now, he could only wait.

Wentworth stripped and flung himself across his bed, but, for a long while, even his powerful will could not drive his harassed mind into the nothingness of sleep. At the end of two hours, he awoke without summons. A cold shower, and a brisk rub-down, and he was as refreshed as from a full night's rest.

But no word had come from Munro—and time passed....

BY A violent exertion of will, Wentworth forced himself to sit quietly in his drawing-room to await that call. His mind would stray... and presently he would find himself striding the floor with long, reaching strides, his hair rumpled from the quick, hard thrusts of his lean fingers through it. Somehow, he should be able to hit on the target of Munro's plans this day. The banks would be closed, and fire was not, anyway, a potent weapon against those structures built conventionally of stone and steel. He gripped his temples hard. Damn it, he could not *think*. But his every nerve was vibrantly alert. He knew that this day Munro would strike!

The day dragged out its weary course. Three times, Kirkpatrick called, but he was asking for information and had none himself to offer. In Wentworth's home, no one moved save on tiptoe. Time and again, Jackson would come to stand silently behind him, but he was not an articulate man. He could not proffer the sympathy he felt. There was a scowling rage on the face of Ram Singh, and Punjabi curses hissed through his lips. Even Jackson, who usually bantered him, did not cross him this Thanksgiving Day.

Blue dusk began to gather in the streets and the western sky held low clouds, red as the flames that Munro raised so terribly—and still there came no word. Wentworth fought against a feeling of helplessness and despair. He knew that all this had been deliberately calculated by Munro; that somewhere in the city he was making his dual preparations, to kill the Spider, and to loot when the hour was ripe. But Wentworth knew that, regardless of the fact that Munro had planned to keep him idle, his greatest hope of finding and destroying this wanton butcher was to do precisely that. When the telephone shrilled….

Old Jenkyns, the butler who had served Wentworth's father before him, came in on silent feet with food… and Wentworth realized that the night had turned black and overcast. It was after nine o'clock. He rose to stretch his taut muscles, and the phone bell whirred again.

Jenkyns started violently, turned with his passive stride toward the phone in the hallway. At Wentworth's crisp signal, Jackson started the sonograph instrument to record the voice, as they had each time the phone bell had sounded. He strained his ears to catch Jenkyns' voice, his hand on the instrument at his side. This was part of a calculated plan to keep whoever called waiting on the wire as long as possible, so that the message could be quickly traced.

Jenkyns was in the doorway of the drawing-room, and the pallor of his face told its own story. Wentworth lifted the phone, and saw with a curious detachment that there was no tremor in his hand. Well, would he expect the long years of training to fail him now?

"Richard Wentworth here," he said quietly.

The instant the man spoke, Wentworth knew with a sharp sense of disappointment that it was not Munro. He pushed out words in a wild hurry.

"In one minute, Wentworth, tune your radio to twenty-three megacycles," he rushed. "One minute… twenty-three megacycles!"

Wentworth said steadily, "Would you mind repeating…" He cut off then, for the man had disconnected. Wentworth came alertly to his feet.

"Ram Singh!" he snapped. "Out on the terrace. Use that directional loop and spot the direction from which that message will come. Jackson, phone the police radio-room direct and get their directional loop working on it. You got the wave-length… twenty-three megacycles!"

Wentworth sprang toward the radio, paid little heed when the telephone shrilled again. That would be the telephone company reporting on the whereabouts of the man who had just called him, and Wentworth knew now that was unimportant.

He might have been sent miles from the hideout to make the call. But Munroe would calculate that he could not trace the radio message without preparation… and he might be right! It was possible that he would speak from a car equipped with two-way radio, and in that case the directional loop would accomplish nothing. If the transmitter were stationary….

Wentworth heard the slow warming of the tubes in his set and stood glowering down at the radio receiver. He tuned it to the specified wave-band. He shifted the sonograph so that he could record the voice that came from the radio and, abruptly, he stiffened. A startled cry leapt from his lips. A voice was coming from the radio.

"Dick!" it called. "Dick! Listen carefully…."

It was the voice of Nita!

"Dick, I am allowed to say only what has been written for

me," she went on steadily, deliberately, "Listen carefully, for I may not repeat."

Wentworth's hands reached out impotently toward the radio. He shook his head, forcing sharp attention on Nita's words as she went on in that same deliberately way.

"These are the orders of Munro," she said. "At precisely nine-thirty, the Spider will enter the end of the Park Avenue traffic tunnel at Fortieth Street, on foot. He will walk through this tunnel to the south end."

Wentworth was only half-listening to the words, though his mind flashed ahead to the picture. That short tunnel, which once had been utilized by street cars, was used now as an auxiliary passage to carry traffic from the Park Avenue ramps that wove around Grand Central Terminal. After dark, it was closed, but only by a series of signs placed across its mouth. In its six blocks of darkness, the Spider must walk, and somewhere inside... he would meet death!

That much was clear, but Wentworth's attention had been caught by something strange in Nita's manner of speech. He was alert for some secret message from her, under the cover of those words; a hope that had sagged dismally when she said she was reading a written message. But there was that strange something in her speech. Some of her words were drawled slowly, but others had a quick staccato delivery. There was a rhythm there....

"If the Spider fails to do this, I am to be killed, Dick," Nita went on, drawling now. "Bu-ut Mu-unro ha-as," Three slow words, now suddenly three swift words, staccato, sharp, *allowed me to* s-a-ay thi-is a-added *thing*. Fo-orget abo-out me-e, *Dick, and don't te-ell the-e Spi-der.* Signing off. Goodnight, dear and… good-by!"

The hum of the radio station died out, and Jackson was instantly on the wire, calling police headquarters, but Wentworth stared before him blankly. Three slow words, three quick words, three slow words. Three dashes… Why, good God, Nita had been signaling in Morse code!

WENTWORTH WHIPPED about to the sonograph and rapidly made the necessary adjustments to repeat the message. Once more Nita's curiously rhythmic voice sounded in his ears… but instead of clearing, Wentworth's bewilderment increased. He knew now that it was in Morse code, her message, and he knew what she had signaled, but it meant nothing, nothing at all.

Nita's secret message was: *"SOS."*

Jackson whipped about from the telephone. "Police got the message. The directional reading is one-eighty—three-sixty."

Ram Singh strode into the drawing-room, his eyes gleaming fiercely. *"Han, sahib,* let us go and destroy them!" he cried. "They are due south of us!"

"Or due north," Wentworth murmured. "You mean that your reading was…."

"One-eighty—three-sixty, *sahib!"*

Wentworth ripped out a harsh oath. Due to some accident, or design on the part of Munro, the two readings had told absolutely nothing of the exact location from which the station had broadcast. A north-south line through police headquarters and his own home would lead out over the water of the harbor and across Staten Island, into New Jersey, Northward... Wentworth whipped about suddenly.

"Jackson, get Kirkpatrick on the phone!" he cried. "Tell him that Munro had access to the room in which the men were questioned, or overheard our conversation in the hallway! He knew that we were going to attempt a sonograph identification, and for that reason he did not send the message to me himself, but had it radioed by Nita! Tell him to make sure that none of Munro's witnesses escaped!"

Wentworth bounded toward his chambers, flinging an order at Ram Singh, "Get over to the pier, and warm up the motor of that seaplane!" he snapped. "Phone Jenkyns a number at which he can call you. Once the motor is warmed, keep it idling and stand by that phone!"

In his room, Wentworth made swift preparations. He snapped two broad rubber bands about his wrist and thrust under them a light, powerful automatic. His eyes were glittering like ice, and he whipped about when Jackson stepped inside the room. Jackson's broad face was set in stony lines.

"Mr. Kirkpatrick had left headquarters, sir," he reported. "I gave the message to Sergeant Reams. Reams was sore as hell, sir. Toley let the witnesses go home for Thanksgiving dinner. Police were sent to guard them... and one of the witnesses murdered his police guard and escaped!"

Wentworth choked down the oath that leaped to his lips. Always just too late! The man had been Munro without a doubt... and they had grasped only another phantom. Give that man ten minutes alone, and he would be a totally different character… He laughed sharply.

"But they will have a sonograph chart of his voice!" he cried. "Jackson, you will stay here and await orders by telephone."

Jackson made no response. His faithful blue eyes looked stubborn. "Begging the Major's pardon, sir," he said stolidly, "Is the Major planning to… walk through that tunnel?"

Wentworth was suddenly very quiet. "Don't be a fool, Jackson," he said calmly. "It is the price Munro has placed upon Miss Nita's life!"

"Does the Major trust Munro?"

Wentworth shook his head, and a slow, grim smile built about his lips. "No, Jackson… but Munro will be there to make sure the Spider dies! He may… find matters not too much to his liking! He worked pretty cleverly, giving me too little time to make preparations to trap him. His own plans are undoubtedly fully arranged!"

Jackson stood very stiffly, "Begging the Major's pardon, sir, I wish to volunteer."

"You what?"

"I wish to volunteer, sir, to… walk through that tunnel." Jackson's eyes burned steadily into Wentworth's. "You know, sir, that it is certain death. You… The Major won't stand a chance!"

Wentworth's eyes softened, and he dropped a hand on Jackson's shoulder warmly. "Thanks, Jackson," he said quietly. "You can serve me best here." His heart swelled at the loyalty of this man who served him, as thoughtless of self as was the Spider in his service to humanity. He shook Jackson's broad shoulder a little. "I've been in these deathtraps before, man, and...."

Jenkyns was at the door suddenly. "Master Richie," he mumbled. "Commissioner Kirkpatrick is here. He wants you at once...."

Wentworth stiffened. He had no time to talk to Kirkpatrick. Minutes were flying... and he had a rendezvous with death.

"Tell him..." he began harshly, and cut off. Kirkpatrick was standing just behind Jenkyns.

"Glad I found you in time, Dick," he said quietly. "I have a favor to ask of you!"

Wentworth moved a hand impatiently. "Any other time, Kirk," he said sharply.

"You heard that radio message from Nita, didn't you? Do you think I can let the Spider *walk* into a trap like that, and not be there to help him?"

Kirkpatrick's blue eyes did not waver at all, and there was grimness in the thrust of his jaw. "The Spider is a law-breaker," he said stolidly. "A killer... I am swearing you in as a deputy, Dick. I am calling on you as an officer of the law demanding the support of a citizen as he has the right to do. "You will help me trap the Spider?"

Wentworth laughed sharply. "You're crazy, Kirkpatrick!" he said violently. "The Spider is risking his life to save Nita! He called me a few moments after that radio message and promised that he would. And you ask me to help trap him? You're mad!"

Kirkpatrick's jaw was stubborn, and his hand moved at his side. Four uniformed policemen stepped into sight beside him, guns in their fists! Wentworth knew then that he would have no choice of refusing! But, damn it, this was his one chance to save Nita, to snare Munro! Suppose he made a break for it, even in the face of those four guns? Then Kirkpatrick would track him down, and arrest him… as the Spider!

And time was flying. Within a little more than twenty minutes, the Spider must start his stroll into that tunnel of death!

"I intend to settle this matter once and for all," Kirkpatrick said harshly. "If you are the Spider, then the Spider cannot appear if you are with me. Dick, you will either do as I say, or I shall clamp you into a cell under protective arrest!"

He frowned. "Well, Dick… which is it going to be? Will you help me trap the Spider, or shall I put you in my private escape-proof cell!"

Wentworth's eyes held the shine of desperation, but his voice was very quiet.

"A man would make but one choice, Kirkpatrick," he said curtly. "Where is this cell of yours?"

CHAPTER 9
HELL BELOW

KIRKPATRICK'S FACE darkened at Wentworth's words, but he did not waver from his resolved purpose. He spoke crisply, and two of the uniformed men sidled into Wentworth's room and moved toward him, guns and handcuffs ready. Wentworth was aware that Jackson was watching narrowly for a signal, and he shook his head slightly. He knew that Kirkpatrick's patience had worn thin. There had been too many recent coincidental appearances of Wentworth on the scene of the Spider's operations. Moreover, Wentworth dared not risk receiving a wound! Too much depended on his remaining ready for the battle. But the time was so cruelly short... Twenty minutes!

"All right," he said angrily, "come on with the handcuffs! Put me in this escape-proof cell of yours, and get on with your trapping of the Spider! If only I had a chance to warn him!"

The police snapped on the handcuffs and Jackson watched with a puzzled air; then resolution formed in his face.

"I'm sure, sir," he said, "that the Spider would expect some such trap as this. I'm quite sure it won't keep him from appearing!"

Wentworth's head whipped toward his man, and he read Jackson's intention in his direct blue gaze. Wentworth's voice still seemed angry. "You will not leave this apartment, Jackson!" he snapped. "I won't have the Spider thinking we are parties to the trap! You understand, Jackson, no matter how badly you wish to help the Spider, you will not leave this apartment—or you will leave my service!"

Jackson's face went pale. His voice was stolid, "Yes, Major!"

Wentworth jerked at the handcuffs, "Come along! Let's see this cell—or you'll be late for your treachery, Kirkpatrick!"

Worry gnawed at the back of Wentworth's brain. Jackson's intention had been completely plain. It had been his intention to don the robes of the Spider—and walk into that tunnel of death, as he had volunteered to do before Kirkpatrick's arrival.

It would be fatal, in more ways than one. Jackson was a grand fighting man, but he lacked the split-second brain of the Master of Men! If he escaped the attack of the criminals, he would surely fall into the hands of the police, and that would be as disastrous as if Wentworth himself were captured in the robes of the Spider!

Wentworth had made the choice of the cell with full knowledge that he might be dooming himself irrevocably. But if he went with Kirkpatrick, there would be no chance at all to appear as the Spider— and Wentworth had not yet given up hope of keeping his rendezvous with death! He

The valice swept across the desk and knocked the telephone to the floor.

maintained a hard silence while the police took him down in the elevator and out where Kirkpatrick's car waited. Wentworth stole a glance at the clock on the dashboard of the car. Already quarter past nine! Fifteen minutes....

"My home," Kirkpatrick told the driver quietly, "and make it fast, Cassidy."

Wentworth said nothing. His eyes bored straight ahead, and the police were close about him, with ready guns. He was tempted to strike out about him; to break from custody and take his chances later with convincing Kirkpatrick that his escape had been made in order to warn the Spider. No, better to wait, until he had seen this escape-proof cell of Kirkpatrick's! Strange that he had ordered the driver to his home... He tried to keep his eyes off the slow jumping of the dashboard clock hands.

Wordlessly still, Kirkpatrick took Wentworth up the elevator to his own apartment, and now they were alone save for the driver, Cassidy. The man's pale blue eyes roved over Wentworth constantly, and Wentworth studied him secretly. Evidently, this man was to be his guard. His hopes rose... One man on guard! **WHEN HE** saw the cell, his heart fell. He remembered now that Kirkpatrick had mentioned once before a plan for safeguarding witnesses against criminal assault; the next time one was threatened, he would keep that witness in his own home! And this cell had been prepared for that purpose. It had no window, and only one door, which opened into Kirkpatrick's bedroom. That door was reinforced by a second gate of tool steel. And the locks were intricate and shielded by a broad plate of armor steel that precluded the possibility of Wentworth reaching it! When the door clanged shut, Kirkpatrick stepped back from the grating, and his eyes pleaded for understanding.

"I have to do this, Dick," he said quietly. "Cassidy, I hold you entirely responsible." He touched a button, and a shield of bullet-proof glass slid out of floor sockets. "You will stand behind this shield, Cassidy," he said. "You will not stir from this spot until I return. Dick, it won't be long. In ten minutes, the Spider will appear... or I will know that you are the Spider!"

"And if anything should prevent the Spider from appearing," Wentworth said quietly, "you will have been responsible for Nita's death! Remember that!"

Kirkpatrick's face was gray and drawn. "The Spider always keeps his word," he said... and strode from the room.

Behind the shield, Cassidy stood rigidly, gun in hand, and his eyes rested a little fearfully upon Richard Wentworth. Wentworth stood motionless also. There was so little time. But, as Kirkpatrick had said, the Spider always kept his word! There had to be a way out. He still had the small automatic strapped to his arm; police had found and removed the others, but that glass shield prevented him from using the gun. Short of Cassidy's death, there was no way he could escape without the knowledge of Kirkpatrick, sooner or later; and that knowledge would be more condemnatory than if the Spider failed to appear! But Nita... God!

Wentworth did not delude himself with the hope that Munro would turn Nita free even if the Spider did appear, but it was his one last chance to make contact with a man as fleeting as a handful of smoke. He had to be there; had to capture Munro... *had to.* Wentworth's eyes were half-veiled by their lids as he studied Cassidy. There was still a way, perhaps. Cassidy was a genius at driving, but Wentworth remembered he had not done so well as a patrolman. Cassidy was frowning now with hard concentration as he gripped his revolver behind the shield.

Yes, Wentworth had one slim chance. He had battled against the will of master hypnotists himself, and had never succumbed unless drugs had been used upon him previously. It was the power of his mind against theirs, and it was the mind of the Master of Men that triumphed. That he had the personal magnitude for command he had proved time and again; every leader has to that extent the potency of the hypnotist. But could he... could he hypnotize Cassidy! Wentworth knew the theory of the art perfectly, though he had not himself practiced it. In the end, it reduced itself to tiring the optic nerves of the patient and overbearing his will power with your own!

Wentworth slipped a key ring from his vest pocket and began to twirl it around and around his finger. It caught facets of bright light, twinkled them against the bullet-proof screen behind which Cassidy stood. He twirled... and presently, he saw that Cassidy's eyes were following the flash of the keys. It was inevitable in a scene so otherwise devoid of interest that he should watch movement. For a long minute after minute, Wentworth twirled the key. Slowly, he lifted his hand toward his face... and Cassidy's eyes followed!

Wentworth waited until the keys were twirling squarely before his own eyes, and then he swallowed the keys with his hand. He had put his own gaze on Cassidy's, and he widened his eyes, concentrated all his will power on holding Cassidy's stare with his own! He saw Cassidy shiver a little; saw him try to look away… and fail!

Wentworth's eyes blazed with the living force of his will, and he flung that thunderbolt of his personality against the weaker mind of the man who confronted him, beyond that screen of glass. Presently, Wentworth's lips began to move, and his sibilant whisper reached across the room.

"My will above yours, Cassidy," he whispered. "My will is stronger than yours. You must obey me! You wish to obey me. Cassidy, you wish to obey me!"

Cassidy's lips quivered. His eyes were strained wide, and the gun was held as solidly as rock in his hand.

"Cassidy!" Wentworth's voice had the command of a trumpet. *"Cassidy, you must obey me!"*

Cassidy's lips moved again. His voice came out woodenly, "I… I must obey you!" he stammered.

Wentworth felt the wetness of perspiration upon his forehead, and he pushed out of his mind all thought other than domination of this man before him. He willed himself to forget the rapid flight of the minutes, and how much that could mean to him.

"We have been fighting men who deal in fire, Cassidy," Wentworth said softly. "They have set this place on fire. You can feel the heat of it. That is why the perspiration is on your forehead. That is why you are afraid, Cassidy. The place is on fire!"

Fright stiffened Cassidy's face. He said, shakily. "The place is on fire!"

"You must release your prisoner, Cassidy," Wentworth whispered. "If you let him burn to death, it would be murder! Kirkpatrick would fire you and you would never drive his car again. You would never again drive a car with the siren shrieking. So you must open the cell, Cassidy. Then you certainly will be a real hero!"

Cassidy went through a struggle then, and Wentworth's eyes burned and burned into his.

"You feel the heat," he said.

"I feel the heat!" Cassidy echoed.

"The place is on fire."

"The place is on fire!"

"Cassidy," Wentworth ordered crisply, "unlock the cell and save the prisoner from the fire!"

Cassidy's lips opened. He shuddered... and stepped slowly around the glass shield. "Unlock the cell," he repeated woodenly!

Seconds later, the steel lattice swung open—and Wentworth stepped outside, a free man! He did not take his eyes from Cassidy.

"Cassidy, behind that glass shield, you will be safe from fire," he said softly. "If you step out from behind it, you will be burned! Stay behind that shield every minute, Cassidy... and *forget what has happened!*"

WENTWORTH BOUNDED across the room, and he staggered a little as he ran, so intense had been the concentration of his mind. He felt as shaken as though he had fought a great battle... and God, time was so short! Impossible now to return to his home for the cape and garb of the Spider! He whirled toward Kirkpatrick's coat closet, and whipped out a long evening dress cape, lined with white satin. He found a black fedora and dragged it down over his brows. It was the best he could do... asbestos cape and fire-extinguishers were at his home. He had one light gun instead of his two heavy arms. And he was going to a rendezvous with almost certain death—to capture the most clever, ruthless criminal he had ever fought!

Wentworth laughed, and the sound came out of his lips with thin self-mockery. He hurled himself down the stairs toward the street. He had three minutes....

Within thirty seconds, Wentworth was hurling himself into a cab at the door of the apartment house.

"Down Park Avenue! Fast!"

The driver wrenched the cab out from the curb and sent it spurting down Park Avenue. Wentworth loosened the gun from the rubber bands at his wrist. The cape was thrown over his arm, the hat perched jauntily on his head. Nothing here for the man to recognize as the Spider! But he could not ride the whole way in this cab, lest a link be made between Kirk's apartment and the rendezvous of the Spider!

A half-dozen blocks down Park Avenue, Wentworth paid off the cab. He waited through feverish seconds while the machine tooled on, then Wentworth turned a corner and stepped toward another cab at the curb. The driver hopped out, and Wentworth moved in sharply. His left fist jolted upward solidly to the jaw, and he crossed the right neatly.

Wentworth stooped over to thrust a ten-dollar bill into the man's hand... then sprang behind the wheel!

One minute was left before he was due to walk into that black tunnel, but it would be enough. A bare ten blocks to cover, and he cared nothing for traffic lights now! As he ground the accelerator to the floor, and felt the stubborn motor begin to catch, a familiar moving figure tagged his glance and his head swung about. He frowned in bewilderment at the thing he saw.

"Kirkpatrick!" he muttered.

He could not be mistaken in that jerky, decisive stride, the commanding aggressive poise of the shoulders. If he needed confirmation, a man in police blue stalked at his elbow! They were going rapidly up the steps and into the lobby of the exclusive Bonheur Hotel.

What business could Kirkpatrick have there at this particular time, Wentworth wondered. He was driving with a wide-open throttle, weaving with sure hands through the dawdling traffic. The lights changed, but Wentworth let the cab rave on. He palmed the horn button and held it down. A cop whistled shrilly, but Wentworth ignored him, raced on. The high entrance to the ramp around Grand Central Terminal was just ahead. Beyond that, across the seven blocks that the viaduct spanned, and he would be at the entrance of the tunnel where he had his rendezvous with death! Yet his thoughts lingered back there with Kirkpatrick. There was an elaborate society ball being held at the Bonheur on this Thanksgiving night. The rich would be there in full panoply of jewels and satins—and he had seen Kirkpatrick enter.

Wentworth jerked his head. He could not think of that now. He must concentrate on the approaching battle. Kirkpatrick's arrival had prevented him using what little time had remained to him for making any plans—for the capture of Munro. He could make none now; charge into the tunnel; locate Munro, and then… Wentworth whipped the cab around the last right-angle turn of the ramp, bore down on the accelerator for the last two-block dash to the entrance of the tunnel. He could see its black cavern arch, the signs set across its mouth to turn traffic aside. Somewhere a clock began to strike out for the half-hour!

The Spider was in time!

Wentworth dragged the cape about his shoulders, pulled the brim of his black hat low over his eyes, and rapidly bound a scarf across the lower part of his face. He gripped his light single gun in his fist, then… and once more bore down on the accelerator!

His eyes stabbed fiercely ahead, and a startled cry crowded out of his throat. As he watched, a cab swerved toward the mouth of the tunnel. Its door whipped open, and from its dark interior, there leaped a figure in a heel-length black cape, with a hat dragged down over its eyes. The figure ran with hunched shoulders, with great black guns gleaming in its fists… and it ran straight toward the entrance of the traffic tunnel.

Another Spider had kept the rendezvous.

Even as Wentworth realized what was happening, that Jackson had defied his explicit orders in order to save Nita and clear Wentworth of suspicion—his eyes flicked beyond the entrance of the tunnel, and he saw another thing that was like a blow between the eyes.

From the shadows of a building entrance, another figure was

racing across the street toward that same tunnel… and it was *Kirkpatrick!*

WENTWORTH'S FOOT faltered on the accelerator, and horror seized him by the throat. He knew now that Munro was not inside the tunnel, and would not come there. His original fear was only too well justified; that Munro would strike with all his ruthless force at some other point while the Spider and police were both concentrating on this one spot.

Without a doubt, Munro had been the man he had seen striding into the Bonheur in the disguise of Kirkpatrick! That meant Munro was going to rob the Bonheur and would turn loose his murdering hordes, his fierce flames upon the hapless thousands who were crowded there tonight!

Only an instant did Wentworth hesitate, yet in that moment he had realized all the horror that sudden, liquid flame would create in that crowded hotel; and he had made his plans! He bore down on the accelerator… and sent the cab roaring straight toward that yawning black tunnel!

The cab struck the traffic standards and leaped high, sent them clattering and broken aside, the noise of the motor was suddenly deafening in Wentworth's ears. He whistled twice, an eerie, piercing note that he and Jackson had used as a signal before this. It would tell Jackson who roared into the tunnel behind him! He heard the whistle shrill back in joyous answer and, as if that had been a signal, hell broke loose there in that tunnel beneath the streets of New York!

In one instant, the entire walls of that tunnel were converted into flame!

Wentworth crouched over the wheel, feeling the shock of the flaming concussion even through the tightly closed windows. The heat reached through with the impact of a hammer blow. He shielded his eyes, and kept the cab rolling. Ahead, he could see the crouched figure of Jackson, a black, tiny huddled thing in the middle of that inferno. But Jackson had drawn over his head, the asbestos-lined cape that the Spider had made with just such a trap as this in mind!

That cape was smoldering on the surface, but even as Wentworth jerked on the brakes, and reached for the door, he saw a hand dart out from beneath the cape—and an area of flame blacked out instantaneously! White fumes swirled upward with the heat, crawled out across the floor, and Jackson wrenched out his hand again, and again, and hurled the flame-extinguishers about him. Wentworth let the cab roll slowly forward into that area of blackness, and Jackson straightened, ran staggering toward Wentworth. The wig of the Spider was singed from his head; the makeup was striped with perspiration, and he was panting between the strangling coughs.

Wentworth hurled open the door and sprang to the pavement.

"One side!" he snapped above the roar of the flames, and the cab trundled forward in second gear, throttle yanked wide. Slowly, it gained momentum. The tires were blazing from the inflammables through which it had raced; spots of paint were flaming on its sides.

Wentworth seized Jackson by the arm and, in a half-dozen

long bounds, reached an emergency exit that led upward by steel ladders to the streets above.

"We will wait here a moment," Wentworth said quietly.

Jackson nodded.

They stood there and their strangling breath filled the narrow way. The roar and heat of the flames was all about them sweeping past the entrance to their cul-de-sac. Munro had done a thorough job of priming the walls with inflammables, so that even the stones seemed to burn. It would not last long, but it would last long enough to wipe out of existence any human being who dared it in ordinary clothing, and with any less powerful extinguisher than the ones that Jackson carried.

Wentworth listened tautly. Jackson said no word, but he had drawn himself up stiffly in his soldier's attitude. Wentworth did not speak to him, but his heart went out to Jackson. He had risked death before in the Spider's name, but this time he had done even more—he had risked being discharged by the master he loved better than life itself! He was waiting now for the blow to fall.

"Robe and hat," Wentworth ordered coldly. "Makeup kit? Good! Follow me!"

Wentworth swept on the robe of the Spider, and slowly, soundlessly, made his way up the escape ladder. When he was half-way up, he heard the crash as the taxi cab, kept straight by the close walls of the tunnel, smacked into the traffic stanchions at the far end of the passage. He heard the sharp shouts of the police, their shrill whistles; even the echo of pounding feet as they raced toward the spot.

"This will have to be fast!" Wentworth whispered to Jackson. "As soon as we are clear of this place, I'm going to expose myself to the police, and lead them away. You will then return to your post, according to orders. Understand this, Jackson?"

Jackson said, woodenly. "Yes, Major! I—"

Wentworth smiled slightly. "You will assemble four automatics, and a dozen hand grenades and await further instructions."

Jackson said eagerly, "Yes, Major!"

WENTWORTH THRUST open the grating and slipped out into the open air. The police guard for this exit was a half-dozen paces away, staring fixedly down the street toward where the taxi was wrecked against a lamp-post, a blazing wreck. Wentworth took two long strides, and his fist crashed against the policeman's jaw. He eased him to the ground, gazed piercingly about him. His lips smiled thinly as he saw Kirkpatrick's car, almost across the street!

In a single lithe movement, Wentworth vaulted the metal fence that girdled the Central park above the traffic tunnel. He was three-quarters of the way across the street before the driver of Kirkpatrick's car saw him, then the man stared open-mouthed through a long moment before he stabbed for his gun. It was too late. Wentworth's fist lashed out again, connected with the man's jaw. Wentworth eased him out of the car, to the pavement, and slid in behind the wheel. He cut the siren loose, started the machine rolling, and executed a swift U-turn.

Police darted out into the street ahead of him, recognized the commissioner's car and hesitated. Kirkpatrick sprang out from a post at the entrance of the tunnel, and Wentworth headed straight toward him… swerved at the last moment.

Wentworth leaned out of the car then, and his scarf-masked face beneath the broad-brimmed black hat was secretly smiling.

"Follow me, Kirkpatrick!" he called, "and I'll lead you to Munro!"

A policeman gasped, *"The Spider! It's the Spider!"*

Then Wentworth drove down on the accelerator and the powerful car of the police commissioner leaped forward and took the ramp back toward upper Park Avenue. The smile that had touched his lips for an instant at sight of the complete bewilderment upon Kirkpatrick's face was gone now, and there was another, grimmer expression. God grant that he would lead the police after Munro in time! This was the swiftest way… for the police to pursue the Spider! They would not be slow to take up this chase!

Wentworth whipped the long limousine through the twisted lane of the viaduct, sent it bellowing down the slope and into Park Avenue. He wrenched the siren wide, and held it that way. His eyes burned ahead to the sedate facade of the Bonheur Hotel. It had been no more than five minutes ago that he had seen Munro, disguised as Kirkpatrick, enter those broad doors. Five minutes… But a thousand men could die in that many seconds! Only, Munro had not yet released his flames upon the hotel. The blow might fall at any moment….

Wentworth swerved the powerful machine and rammed straight toward a red box, set upon a standard on the corner—a red fire-alarm box! The front bumper caught it, slammed it straight down upon the pavement. The box split into fragments, bounced high… and Wentworth was racing on! That was one way to turn in a fire-alarm, and he had no time to stop! He had killed the siren. The police behind him were getting under way. The first two radio cars dived down the chute of the viaduct with their sirens shrieking like women in pain. Wentworth clipped one more fire-box, and then he swung the limousine in a whistling curve and slammed it to the curb in front of the Bonheur Hotel!

With a single long stride, he was across the sidewalk while the stupefied doorman still stared. He went up the steps in a bound, batted his way through the revolving doors… and bounded to the middle of the lobby!

A woman was smiling, leaning her shoulders against one of the marble columns as she looked up into the face of her escort. She frowned at the sudden cold that the Spider's swift entrance had brought, and turned her head. She screamed then, and pointed with a shaking hand. She screamed, "The Spider!"

A half dozen, then a score, then a hundred voices echoed that shout. Men and women were suddenly running from the lobby of the hotel! But Wentworth threw both arms high above his head, and his voice rang out clearly.

"Listen to me," he cried. "Listen to the Spider, and know that the Spider does not lie! This place is going to be robbed tonight, perhaps within a few minutes! The robbers will set the building on fire. The police and the fire department are on the way. Be calm… Do not allow yourself to be stampeded!"

Hard-faced men wedged suddenly out of a narrow corridor to

the left of the lobby, pounded toward him with hands reaching for their guns. Wentworth knew them for the squad of detectives maintained by the hotel.

"This way!" he shouted to them.

With an easy vault, Wentworth cleared the marble counter of the desk. His weight smashed against the staring clerk, carried him to the floor.

Wentworth crouched beside the terrified man. "Commissioner Kirkpatrick came in here a moment ago," he said harshly. "Where is he?"

The clerk's eyes rolled up. "The manager!" he gasped. "The manager… His office!"

His quivering hand pointed toward a door at one end of the desk alcove and Wentworth sprang toward it. A gun crashed from the lobby and he heard the deathly whisper of the lead past his head. He hit the door—and it was locked. No time for finesse now that the alarm was given! Wentworth's gun cracked twice in his hand, shattering the lock, and the drive of his shoulder hurled it quivering inward. His leap carried him two-thirds of the way across the office, and the smashing detonation of a gun greeted him; his automatic answered and a man in police blue stepped backward a half-pace. His head was punched backward so that he seemed, incredulously, to stare at the ceiling. Then his uniform hat slipped off and bounced on the floor, and his body let loose all at once. He slumped forward to the floor, a bullet hole between his eyes.

In a single all-inclusion glance, Wentworth took in the manager's office. A man in evening dress lay sprawled upon the floor with a bullet-hole through the back of his skull. The safe gaped, and papers were strewn about... and a man was just rising with a valise stuffed full of money from before the looted strongbox. At the swift double crash of the guns, he whipped about—and Wentworth gasped!

Even when he knew the truth, when his unfaltering gunhand was sweeping up for the final shot that would wipe Munro from the face of the earth, he felt a shock run along his nerves. In that first, curt glance, he would have sworn he was gazing into the face, and the eyes, of Commissioner Stanley Kirkpatrick!

It required a conscious effort to force his hand to close on the trigger, and Wentworth knew even as he fired, that he had missed! Great God, the Spider, face-to-face with a mass murderer, had missed an easy shot! His body had refused the clear order of his brain, because of the shock that Munro's resemblance to Kirkpatrick had given him. For once the Spider's highly-trained reflexes had played him false! There was time for no second shot!

Wentworth saw mockery leap into those dark eyes that stared so fixedly into his. The valise swept across the desk, and knocked the telephone to the floor—*and the room exploded!*

WENTWORTH FELT heat strike him like a moving wall. It plucked him from the floor and hurled him backward. Somehow, he managed to whip the asbestos-lined cape before his face, but the shock, the heat, almost overpowered him. Half-dazed through he was, he drove himself to his feet, fought his way through the swirling smoke, the leaping tongues of crimson flame. The gun quested like a hound's nose for its prey, and did not find it. Behind him, he could hear the sudden screams of people, and he knew that the touch-off of the entire hotel had been hooked up with some electrical contact connected with the telephone. Munro's sweeping valise, loaded with loot, had set off a holocaust!

Wentworth smashed two of the flame-extinguishers against the walls of the office, and then he could see an open door across its width. He hesitated, not in fear of what might lie behind, but with a divided sense of duty. All his being urged him to fling himself in violent pursuit of Munro now, while he knew in what guise the man fled. But there were hundreds, thousands of people trapped in the hotel. Wentworth hesitated... and there came to his ears the screams and shrieks of a dozen sirens. He heard the hoarse, long-drawn wail of the fire-engines; the whimpering, yelping thinness of police radio cars; the deeper ululation of the ambulances.

Wentworth laughed harshly. Between their eagerness to catch the Spider, and his own care to summon the fire department, there would be ample help for the people of the hotel within a space of seconds.

The Spider was free to hunt!

With that laugh, Wentworth thunder-bolted across the room and burst out through that closed door. A gun hammered furiously from the darkness at a corridor's end, a man was emptying a gun as fast as he could pull the trigger... and that was no way to shoot accurately, as Wentworth could have told him. He threw a shot across his chest toward that nickering snake-tongue of powder-flame... and it was extinguished. The Spider javelined. At least, after that first moment did not even pause. He bounded toward where a gleam of street lights showed an exit, whipped to the street!

A car was spurting from the curb and Wentworth's automatic lifted with deadly perfection toward the driver, who wore still the neatly formal derby that Kirkpatrick affected in winter— and then Wentworth swore, and did not fire! He had caught the yellowish green gleam of lights across the glass of the limousine, and knew that his bullet would be wasted. Bulletproof!

There was a crowded taxi rank, and Wentworth lunged toward the nearest cab, flung into the front seat beside the driver.

"After that car!" he ordered, and the cold incisiveness of his voice snapped the man from the lethargy of waiting. He jammed in the gear while his eyes flinched from the gaunt, caped figure beside him, from the cold glint of the gun in the Spider's hand.

Wentworth said quietly, "Wreck that car ahead! And don't worry about your job, or this cab. I'll pay for the machine, and give you a thousand-dollar bonus… *But wreck that car ahead!*"

The taxi leaped under the spur of the Spider's words, but the limousine already had a block lead. Wind drummed violently against the cab, hit it at the corners like a mighty sledge. Traffic skittered aside as the horn blared for right-of-way through red lights. Wentworth's eyes burned in his head. The scarf muffled him to the nose, and his hands were calm upon the gun. He slipped out the clip, fingered the bullets. Two shots left, and one in the chamber. A weak armament with which to tackle Munro! He could not waste bullets in chance shots at this high speed. And there was too much traffic. A stray bit of lead, a ricochet….

"He's got a fast car, boss," the driver gasped. He was panting, his face streaked with perspiration. His eyes darted everywhere and the cab dodged like a rabbit. The limousine ahead took no such precautions. It slammed straight through—across Broadway, across Eighth, boring steadily westward!

Wentworth shook his head, thinking fiercely. In a short while, the man must turn either north or south. If he hit the westside elevated highway, he would walk away from this cab. Their chance would come on the turn. Wentworth reached out and cranked down the right-hand window. The cold struck through the opening like a knife. Wentworth tugged his hat down firmly over his temples, knotted the scarf fast about his face and leaned out. He was crouching, countering the jars of their speed with flexed knees; ready to shoot....

A cry leaped to his lips! Ignoring the blare of that screaming horn ahead, a small car pushed out across the intersection with Ninth Avenue. Too late, the girl who was driving saw the juggernaut of the limousine, tried to turn two ways at once... and clapped her hands over her eyes in despair. The limousine swerved a foot, caught the small car on the right rear wheel. The coupé looped, turned over, slammed upside down into an elevated pillar. The limousine was past... but the coupé was not through! It bounced from the pillar, fell to its side and spun slowly around—directly into the path of the taxi!

THE CAB driver stood on the brakes. He was half-erect, crouched behind the wheel. He flung the cab into a twisting turn to the right, and the tires screamed, skated across the wet pavement. He countered the skid with a wrench of the wheel, caromed off an elevated pillar with a shriek of torn metal. Glass showered across the front seat from a shattered window… and then the cab was roaring northward along Ninth Avenue.

"Left again!" Wentworth ordered coldly. "I'll double that bonus! That man deliberately hit the girl's coupé. Deliberately, I tell you—to stop us!"

The driver's jaw was set and he whipped to the left, fought the car out of the skid, and floored the accelerator.

"Gawd A'mighty," he said. "Gawd *A'mighty!* She wasn't even screaming. She…."

Wentworth shook his head. There was a stinging in his eyes, and a fury in his heart. If he lost the trail this time… Damn it, he could not lose the trail! That poor girl in her shattered coupé. He had seen her at the last moment there. Seen her with the steering-post thrust through her frail body like a brutal, blunt javelin. At least, after that first moment of fright, she had not suffered. By God, Munro should suffer!

And there was Nita….

The taxi was hammering down the last straight stretch toward West Street where the elevated highway ran. No entrance at this corner, or the one below. At any moment, he should see the limousine flash past. Wentworth weighed his gun. Not a chance of hitting it in the brief while it would be exposed. He sat tensely forward and his hands fondled the gun.

"Must have turned south!" the driver shouted.

Wentworth nodded wordlessly, braced himself. The cab hit the smooth, shining pavement in a broadside skid, writhed between two of the highway supports and straightened out.

Wentworth strained his eyes ahead... Dear God, the street was empty!

Somewhere in those last few blocks, Munro had twisted aside, or else... or else he had driven straight into one of the piers that lined the water's edge! Wentworth's gaze whipped toward the docks and then, above the high hammer of the cab's motor, he caught another sound. It was a deep-throated roar, and there was a blustering quality to that tone that he recognized! Behind the walls of those piers, a seaplane was taking off!

"That pier!" Wentworth shouted, and pointed.

The cab broad-sided again, lashed across the width of West Street toward the broad doors of the pier. They had been open, but they were closing now, closing swiftly. Wentworth thrust out his body through the window and leveled the automatic. He saw a hand, white against the edge of the sliding doors, squeezed the trigger once!

The hand jerked out of sight—and the door did not close any farther!

"Straight through! Fast!" he snapped.

The cab jounced violently at the short ramp, lunged through the opening. A machine-gun chattered viciously from the darkness but it came an instant too late. The car was already inside... and Wentworth's gun swiveled and blasted! The pale violent flicker of the machine-gun swept upward, higher... higher until it pointed at the zenith. Then it stopped... and the driver was standing on his brakes. The cab's tires howled on the wooden floor.

"Lie down!" Wentworth threw at the driver. "Lie down flat and don't move!"

His door was already open and the Spider vanished with his first long leap into the black shadows that clustered thickly against the walls. If he made any sound at all, it was swallowed in the deep bellowing of the airplane engine. There was a narrow door open to the water, and the glisten of the grayer night came through. Across that opening, a black shadow flitted… and then, just outside on the water's edge, Wentworth checked. He had one bullet left in that light gun in his fist. One bullet… and the plane was already almost completely out of range now!

There was no time to delay. Wentworth could not see the pilot, shielded behind the crash-pad in the cockpit. But he knew this type of plane, knew where its gas tank was! Wentworth squeezed off his last bullet… and the plane charged on, tipped up on the pontoon step, and began its rush to the final take-off. It whirled northward into the wind, and the sound of the motor dwindled, became louder as the plane lifted against the sky. Wentworth stood for a long minute and watched the flicker of the exhaust as the ship climbed steadily.

Now….

Wentworth stared, and slowly a hard smile moved the lips beneath the scarf mask. Nita had signaled SOS and the password that Munro had given in the offices of No-More-Fires, Inc., had been "From my ashes, I arise again!"

Wentworth's lips parted in the harsh, mocking laughter of the Spider. He whipped back inside the pier, and raced for the taxi.

"Get me to a telephone," he told the driver softly, "and then get me to Pier Seventy on the East River as fast as this cab will go." He laughed again, and there was triumph in the sound. "Tonight, Munro dies!"

Death....

He flung himself into the cab, but the smile was no longer on his mouth, and there was a touch of fear in his gray-blue eyes as the taxi whined in a U-curve and spurted for the doors. Tonight, Munro would die, but... would he die in time to save Nita? Nita....

CHAPTER 10
MUNRO'S KNIFE

IN THE tight, small room in which Nita had been imprisoned day and night since her capture by Munro, she paced with quick, controlled steps. She still wore the evening dress of ivory satin, a gown of Grecian simplicity exquisitely molded to her body. The long skirt switched from side to side behind her slim ankles and her narrow white hands were clasped rigidly before her. Her violet eyes did not see the glistening white walls about her.

An hour now had passed; an hour since she had phoned that message to Dick over the radio with a pistol held against her skull. She had been able to do so little to warn him, to tell him the hideout of Munro, but it had been all she had dared. Fortunately, Munro had not been beside her at the time, or she might not have succeeded as well as she had! If only she had dared to blurt out the truth to Dick! She shook her head, laid her wrist against her forehead, and wearily thrust up her chestnut curls. No, that would not have done either. If those men had known she was signaling Dick her whereabouts, then she would have been moved....

Nita checked her swift pacing to stare fixedly at the wall. "Don't be a fool, Nita," she whispered to herself. "There is no hope!"

It was not that she doubted Dick, or his strength, but Munro had taken great delight in detailing to her the trap into which Dick would walk. She did not see how even his superb mind and body could save him. When it was over, Munro had promised her, he would come back... and 'execute' her!

Nita's head sagged slowly forward, and she dropped to her knees on the floor. Perhaps she prayed, but certainly it was not for herself. When she spoke, it was a dear name that was on her lips, *"Dick!"*

Time dragged on wearily, and twice Nita lifted her head, thinking that she had heard the deep approaching hum of an airplane motor. She knew that Munro was using a plane tonight. When he returned... Nita's breast lifted in a slow, taut breath. Why, then, there would be an end of worrying! If only she had been able to tell Dick more, she might hope. But she knew only that she was on a large yacht. No glimpse outside of her state-room had been vouchsafed her, but she could feel the lift and swell of the sea beneath the keel, and hear the mewling of gulls, and distant sob of whistles. There was a bell-buoy somewhere near that she could hear, mournfully clanging, when the wind was right.

167

The Spider's automatics were speaking with crisp deliberation.

A feeble clue, but her SOS meant danger at sea. Dick would recognize that. Beyond that, she must depend on his keen brain—if he were still alive!

Presently, Nita heard shouts on the deck of the yacht, heard the splashing and the drumming of a motor as a launch was lowered to the water. After a while, it returned, and it was not long afterward that she heard the key turn in the lock of the door. Nita rose slowly to her feet; her chin lifted, and she stood that way when the door was flung wide.

Two men stood either side of the door in the narrow corridor, and facing her was... Munro!

AS ALWAYS at sight of that flame-seared face, those distorted eyes and mouth that seemed perpetually twisted in a savage leer, Nita could not repress a shudder. She saw amusement glisten in the eyes.

"You are quite right, *mamselle*," Munro said, with a calm that was gloating. "The time has come for you to be... executed. Come!"

Munro stepped aside, and the eyes of the four men were upon her. Nita's head lifted, and a disdainful smile touched her lips. As calmly as if she answered an invitation to dinner, Nita stepped across the raised sill of her stateroom and turned left along the corridor behind Munro. The men fell in about her in a square and the march of their feet made a regular soft thudding to the sharp rap of her own high heels. Nita felt coldness about her heart... but it was despair, not fear.

If Munro returned, it meant that Dick had... failed!

The corridor ended in a tight little salon and Munro turned

sharply to the right, dropped into a chair that was isolated like a throne. But for the moment, Nita's eyes did not rest on him. The salon had been changed since the time, only a brief hour or two before, she had been marched through it to broadcast that warning to Dick. There was no furniture in it at all, except that lonely chair and… and what stood opposite it!

Nita drew in a slow, quivering breath as she saw the way she was to die, and afterward did not look at the thing at all. She did not need to. It was engraved forever in her mind. Her lips twisted a little. For her, 'forever' might be so brief a while!

A narrow tower of old stained wood had been erected against the wall. It was wedged tightly between ceiling and floor, and there was a knife between its side-beams—a knife that was a triangle of glistening steel, sharpened to a razor edge and heavily weighted above. Munro had erected a guillotine!

The bulkhead behind it had been draped in canvas, and there was another strip spread beneath the guillotine itself. Nita could not repress a shudder. She knew the reason for those strips of canvas. When the knife fell….

Munro chuckled. "I see you get the picture very completely, my dear," he said.

Nita's head came up and her eyes rested scornfully upon the hateful, scarred face of the man in the chair. There were other men in the room now. Nine of them lined the wall behind the chair, and there were guns in their hands. Munro, too, held a gun in his right hand… Suddenly, Nita laughed!

"He escaped!" she said breathlessly. "You set your elaborate trap, and he walked into it as he said he would… but he escaped!

171

And Munro, you are afraid! That is why you have guns in your hands!"

Emotion twisted the man's distorted mouth horribly, and his voice came out in a feral snarl. "Yes, the dog escaped!" he said harshly. "And he cheated me out of three-quarters of my loot for this night! He pursued me through the streets and put a lucky bullet through the gas-tank of my plane, so that it was wrecked. But I had time to call to my men by radio and have the boat lowered! He did all these things… and yet he shall not long enjoy even that partial triumph. Do you know why, you pretty fool?"

"Why, yes," Nita said quietly. "I know why. You intend to kill me." But the smile did not leave her lips. She even laughed a little, lightly. "Do you think you can harm me now? You did not kill him, and that is all that matters. You are doomed, you and all your men!" She shrugged her smooth round shoulders slightly. "You say I am to die. It does not matter. For I know that I shall be quickly avenged!"

Munro leaned sharply forward in his chair, and the rage was a living black fire in his eyes, but his voice came out softly. "As to that, we shall see," he said softly, "but just now I am more interested in your own brief future. My executioner will be here soon. He is arraying himself, for as you know I like things to be just so. Your executioner will wear formal clothing, my dear, and you will not mind if he wears a black hood? It pleases me to have him dress so."

Nita smiled. She no longer saw these men. Hope that would not die sang in her heart. So long as Dick was alive….

"I think that is very nice of you, Munro," she said, in condescension.

Munro jerked to his feet. "I have made some other... nice arrangements!" he snapped. "You have already perceived that the drop of the knife will be shorter than is customary. I have compensated for that by a sharper angle of the blade, and extra weight. There is another little device which I rather like. When the plank to which you are strapped drops into place, there will be no delay. It will automatically release the knife! To compensate for the loss of those few seconds of anticipation, my dear, I have arranged for you... to watch the knife fall! When you are strapped to the plank, it will be face-up! But try to keep your features composed, my dear, for when you are dead, I shall deliver you back to this lover of yours! Your body will be shipped to Richard Wentworth! Your body—and of course, your head!"

NITA FOUGHT the panic that spurted into her brain. She could not let herself think of the horror this man painted, lest she give him the satisfaction of showing her fear. She clung to her smile... and heard footsteps on the deck behind her.

"Ah, my executioner!" said Munro.

Nita turned then, stately as any Marie Antoinette facing the tumbril, and looked at the figure of the man who was to take her life. As Munro had said, he was clothed in formal evening dress, but it fitted him very badly. The black hood hung loosely about his throat, and eyes peered out at her from two slits that shadowed them darkly.

Nita kept the quiver from her voice, "Whenever you are ready," she said quietly.

The executioner was bending now over the plank, examining the straps. It was hinged to an extension of the foot of the platform, and Nita found herself examining it with an awful fascination. She would be strapped to that plank. A thrust would drop her backward, held immovable by those straps. When the plank slapped home between those two slides that guided the knife, then... then the blade would drop! Nita closed her eyes, felt that she swayed a little on her feet. The executioner moved toward her. She heard his feet, felt his hand touch her arm.

Nita was beside the upright plank. At the touch of the gentle hand on her arm, she turned her back to it. God, it was only seconds now. Seconds... Dick, *Dick!*

The sound was forced from her lips, and it seemed to her that in the fury of her desperation she had heard an answer.

"Courage, dear!"

She said, "I am ready!"

Nita had stiffened her body into a kind of cataleptic trance, and what happened then registered on her mind only dimly. It seemed to her that she heard a shattering explosion, and sharp cries. And then she was hurtling backward!

Nita's eyes flew wide, and terrified, lifted toward the knife. In a split-second of time it would be swooping toward her throat! She stared... and did not see the knife! She struck the floor, and her hands flew up and she realized that she was not strapped to that slaughterous plank at all. She had fallen... to the floor!

While this incredible realization was flashing through her mind, she heard *laughter.*

It was a hard and terrible sound, instinct with menace, flat with mockery, but Nita heard it with a joy that seemed to swell her heart to bursting. A sob lifted to her lips, for that laughter... *it was the laughter of the Spider!*

NITA TWISTED her head then and saw what was happening in the room. Not a full second had passed. Those nine men had whipped about toward the door aft, where the explosion had sounded. Their guns were lifting that way. Munro had sprung from his chair, with his automatic ready in his fist. But that open doorway framed only blackness... and the laughter of the Spider came... *It came from the executioner!*

Even as Nita realized that fact, the executioner whipped off his black hood and the bold, chiseled lines of the Spider's face were exposed. There was an automatic in each fist, and the laughter poured from his lips.

"This is the end, Munro!" he shouted.

Munro came to his feet, but in that same instant, death reached out its hot hand for the Spider!

Wentworth saw that Munro thrust down hard with his right foot, and guessed that he stood over some prepared trap. He tried to fling himself strenuously aside, and even the lightning-fast reflexes of the Spider were not swift enough to escape the hell that blossomed beneath him!

Flames fanned up beneath his feet, hot with the breath of the explosion that fathered it. In the same instant, he felt something brush past his face, strike against his arms. From overhead had dropped a hangman's noose!

But this time, Wentworth already was in motion, and triumphant laughter burst mockingly from his lips! His left hand

175

snaked upward and clamped home about that rope, even as it snapped taut! By the sheer muscular power of that one-handed grip, Wentworth wrenched himself upward, and the rope missed his throat—but bound his gun hand to his side! And Munro was leaping toward him, the mad lust to kill glistening in his distorted eyes!

In the bight of the rope, his gun hand still bound at his side, Wentworth flung himself into action! Deliberately, he swayed back over that blossoming hell of flame that had burst beneath him. The hot draft swept up witheringly into his face, whipped his cape bravely. But Wentworth had achieved what he wanted. He got his feet against the bulkhead, and drove himself violently toward Munro!

An inarticulate cry burst from Munro's lips, his gun jerked up—but the Spider was too swift for him! The Spider's feet lashed out and caught Munro in chest and jaw, drove him violently away from where Nita swayed against that fateful guillotine. As Munro fell, Wentworth wrenched free his gun-arm, and began to shoot!

His first bullet raked upward above his head—and cut the rope! Even before it fell free from about him; even before his feet struck the floor, the Spider's automatics were speaking with the crisp deliberation of gunbeats on parade. At each bark of sound, a man crumpled. The man beside Munro's throne jumped backward like a man who has stepped upon a snake, but it was not a voluntary action. Lead had plucked into his belly, and he folded as he was hammered backward through the air. He struck the bulkhead behind him and, afterward, he bent slowly forward until his knees plumped to the floor. He stayed that way, with his forehead grinding into the deck.

A single lithe spring put Wentworth astride Munro's crumpled body.

"Drop your guns!" the Spider ordered.

One man defied that order. One man tried to wrench his gun about to bear upon the Spider as he crouched there. The Spider's eyes did not shift, did not appear to see him, but the gun in his left hand jerked against his wrist, and a shell clattered to the floor. The crash was single, rolling and loud. The man who tried to throw his gun on the Spider wrenched violently backward, lifted on his toes. His head struck a pane of porthole glass and shattered it, and afterward he sat down. Through perhaps twenty seconds, he sat there braced against the bulkhead, though he was already quite dead with a bullet through his head. Then he pitched sideways and moved no more. With his fall, the flare-up of rebellion died. The guns thudded to the floor, and Jackson came in steadily through the doorway, guns in his fists.

"Tie them up," Wentworth ordered calmly. He stirred Munro with his foot, and the man's body flopped limply.

"Can you come here, Nita?"

Nita's voice came hesitantly. "I think so… Of course!" And then he heard her scream!

WENTWORTH WHIPPED about. His gun swung up, but the flitting figure that darted across the room moved too swiftly… and Nita was just beyond! Wentworth leaped to the attack, but he was a split-second too late! Munro had been shamming those last few seconds, and now he was crouched behind Nita. He had her arms vised between his hands... and she was pressed against the upright plank of the guillotine!

"Don't move, you fool," Munro's voice struck strongly through the room, "or I'll throw her against this plank! The knife trigger will be sprung and... Nita will be without a head!"

Nita stood rigidly in the grasp of the man, and Wentworth swore beneath his breath. He had been criminally careless, but he had struck hard enough to crack the man's skull! Of course! Munro, the artist in disguise, had altered the shape of his skull also... with padding! That padding had saved him from the Spider's lethal blow!

"Drop your guns!" Munro snapped. "Spider, if you move again, the girl dies!" he warned. "You forget there is a mirror in the ceiling!"

Wentworth's eyes lifted and the bitterness of despair raked through him. In the mirror that formed the lower surface of a skylight, Munro's evil distorted face grinned back at him. There was triumph there, and an evil gloating.

Wentworth's face twisted with anger. "You are the fool, Munro!" he rasped. "Two things betrayed you, and both of them were caused by your vanity. You do not credit other people with having brains!"

"Certainly not!" Munro snarled. "For the last time, drop that gun!"

Wentworth's lips were cold against his teeth. There was a chance, just one chance, and it would risk Nita's life; it would entail the finest shooting of a lifetime, and he could not take aim. It must be a snapshot. There was a flat metal plate bracing the foot of the guillotine. If he could bounce a bullet off of that at precisely the right angle, it should… knock Munro's legs out from under him!

"I said you underestimated your enemies, Munro!" Wentworth rushed on. "In your office, you gave a password that was sheer folly. You were laughing to yourself when you did it, weren't you, Munro? You said, 'From my ashes, I arise again!' When I figured out that the whole meeting you had called was a trap, I knew that password could not have been pre-arranged, but sprung to your mind spontaneously. Therefore, it was connected with something that was very prominent in your mind at the time."

"Are you almost through, Spider?" Munro asked coldly.

"Almost," Wentworth acknowledged, "and then you allowed Nita to broadcast to me, and she broke her words into a rhythm that duplicated Morse code—she signaled *SOS!* From that moment, I knew she was at sea somewhere, since that is a sea-call of distress. And then I remembered your password… And I knew that you had given a charade for the name of your yacht!

" 'From my ashes, I arise again' obviously meant that legendary bird, the Phoenix, and it fitted in with your macabre sense of humor that, using arson as a means of crime, you should call your yacht after the fire-bird, the *Phoenix.* That was a help, but it was that one bullet I fired which trapped you, Munro—the bullet that I fired, deliberately, through your gas tank!

"It was a leak that would force you down ultimately," Wentworth said quietly. "You kept your motor turning over, so there could not have been too much gas in your tanks. Consequently, you would have to call to your yacht, the *Phoenix*, for assistance. When you called, I was aloft in my own seaplane. I heard a call for the *Phoenix*, and I ran down the bearing with my radio. After that, it was simple. Just as it is going to be simple to kill you, Munro, for you see, Nita has had special training. She had not flinched under your hands, nor moved. In just a moment, Munro...."

Nita's eyes flared wide, and Wentworth knew that she had caught his instruction... and Wentworth squeezed the trigger of the gun. It jerked against his wrist, and Wentworth hurled himself forward in the same instant. He saw the white splash as the lead glanced from the metal plate at which he had aimed. And then... and then, Nita wrenched her body sideways. It was a *jiu-jitsu* throw over the hip, the use of the special training Wentworth had given her long ago; which he had prompted her to use with his few swift words!

Wentworth's gun was ready as Nita wrenched Munro sideways, but he did not fire again. It was not necessary! The ricocheting had batted Munro's legs out from beneath him, and Nita's throw did the rest. She staggered aside, but Munro went back-first against the plank of the guillotine! It swung smoothly downward in its slot, downward beneath the knife!

Munro screamed. He writhed, and tried to throw himself sideways from that plank, but there was no time. At the last moment, as the plank slammed down on the trigger, he flung up his arms in a frantic effort to ward off the swoop of death—and that, also, was too late! The knife swooped down, the knife with

its extra angle and its extra weight to make up for the short-
ness of the drop. A hand thudded to the floor. Munro twisted
his head aside... and the knife slapped home into its groove, its
swift drop finished. There was a thud from beyond the guillotine, and Wentworth gathered Nita protectively into his arms.

Jackson spoke from the doorway, "Prisoners all accounted
for, sir! The plane is moored to the stern, and the folding rubber
boat you used is aboard. Pardon me, sir, but you'll have to hurry!"

Wentworth set Nita from him, "The deck aft, dear," he
murmured. He bent over the guillotine, and on the blade he
affixed the glistening scarlet seal of the Spider. And he looked
beyond the guillotine and his face twitched a little as he turned
away. Because Munro had not been strapped to the plank, the
knife had not struck in quite the right position. No one would
ever know now what Munro's real face looked like....

MINUTES LATER, the seaplane whirled into the wind
and took off under the guidance of Jackson's expert hands.
Rapidly, Wentworth explained about Kirkpatrick's action, and
how he had escaped from the cell in Kirkpatrick's home.

"Kirkpatrick has been violently busy ever since that time!" he
said somberly. "There is just a chance that I can get back before
he does. If I fail... I'm afraid I will have to become a fugitive!"

Nita's hand closed tightly on his. "What do you want me to
do, Dick?"

Wentworth told her quickly, and the plane roared toward
Manhattan. And presently, the ship swooped low with an idling
motor and Wentworth climbed out on a wing, and pulled the
ripcord of his parachute and let the pressure of the wind pull

him off into space. He could steer the parachute by spilling air from one side or another, and the blustering wind of the earlier night had stilled.

NITA FOUND Kirkpatrick leaning wearily upon his desk at headquarters, and she thrust by the door guards haughtily, sailed into Kirkpatrick's inner office.

Kirkpatrick's head snapped up. He staggered to his feet, and his smile was joyous. "Nita! Thank God! How did you get free from that devil! Thanks to the Spider, he didn't do much damage at the Bonheur. No lives lost, except that of the manager, and a couple of criminals that the Spider evidently killed."

Nita lifted a shoulder, "The Spider set me free," she said impatiently. "I was being held prisoner on a yacht and the Spider flew out there and killed Munro and some other men, tied up the rest and flew me back to New York... And I want to know when you're going to turn Dick loose from that ridiculous cell of yours!"

"If Dick is still in that cell," he said, "and Cassidy has been faithful to his trust...."

Nita said, acidly, "I thought this was an escape-proof cell!"

Kirkpatrick shook his head and said no more. He did not expect to find Wentworth in the cell. That, he knew, was the real reason why he had forgotten about Cassidy and his charge. For he had seen the Spider in action, and he had the Spider to thank that a hundred or more lives had not been snuffed out in the Bonheur fire. But, even in his life-saving, the Spider had killed two men!

Kirkpatrick found himself feverishly impatient, so that

he darted ahead of Nita into the apartment house before he thought, and his apology was perfunctory.

From the locked cell door, Wentworth called out angrily, "Kirkpatrick, if you don't let me out of this damned cell, I'm going to sue you so fiercely you'll be kicked out of office. Damn you, can't you understand, Nita is in the hands of Munro, and...."

Nita came into the room then and Wentworth broke off with a glad cry and Nita ran to his arms. He clasped her through the steel bars, and Kirkpatrick heard her telling him rapidly the same things she had told him previously. His eyes were burning into Cassidy's, but the policeman met them steadily.

"Cassidy," he said sharply, "have you been out from behind this glass shield!"

Cassidy sighed, "Faith, Commissioner, I haven't moved, but it's hard on my feet. You didn't give me a chair!"

Kirkpatrick frowned. "In other words, your eyes have never been off Wentworth, and he has not left that cell!"

Cassidy frowned, too. "Never a wink have I taken, Commissioner," he said, "and Wentworth has been standing right there where he is now the whole time!"

Kirkpatrick swung about toward Wentworth, took the keys from Cassidy. There was something that troubled him, and he could not place it. Cassidy had spoken with a straight-forward conviction, and plain sincerity. And yet... Damn it, he had *seen* the Spider! He unlocked the door of the cell.

"It seems, Dick," he said slowly, "that I owe you more apologies than I can ever muster up the words to speak. Tonight, I have seen the Spider with my own eyes, and I know that man in action. It could not have been someone else in disguise. And I had provided you with an unbreakable alibi." He smiled suddenly, and it lighted all his weary face. "Dick, from the bottom of my heart, I am glad! Now, there can be an end of fencing and pretense between us! Will you shake hands?"

Wentworth's heart gave him a twinge. He hated thus to deceive his friend, but his duty and his service to humanity demanded it. He clasped Kirkpatrick's hand warmly... and from the other room, the radio was suddenly loud.

"Attention, Kirkpatrick!" it called sharply. "Kirkpatrick, are you listening. This is the Spider speaking!"

Kirkpatrick smothered an oath and leaped to the doorway. Jackson was standing by the radio. He stammered, "I... I just wanted to see what the news was saying about the Spider," he said.

Kirkpatrick gestured him to silence.

"Kirkpatrick," came the flat and mocking voice of the Spider, "I have done your work for you once more. You'll find Munro dead, and his men, some dead, and some prisoners, on the yacht *Phoenix* anchored off the Coney Island bell buoy about a mile. Also, you will find a sonograph record of his declaration that Nita van Sloan was to die, and why. If you will check it with those I understand Wentworth had you make of certain suspects, you should have no difficulty in making sure that it was Munro speaking!

"And you can do me a favor, Kirkpatrick. Munro seems to make the same mistake that so many of you confounded imbeciles make. He confuses me with Wentworth. Now admittedly,

Wentworth is a superior mentality, but he cannot compare with me! I always… beat him to the kill!

"Do this little thing for me, Kirkpatrick, and give this sop to my vanity! Wentworth… *phooey!*"

Wentworth said violently, "Confound his impudence! He can boast! And here I was, sealed up in a cell…."

Nita said, gently, "But he saved my life, Dick!"

Wentworth grumbled into silence, shrugged. What he muttered sounded suspiciously like, "The conceited ass!"

Kirkpatrick was smiling, and there seemed to be years taken from his shoulders. "I will make that clear for the Spider," he laughed, "and for you, Dick! To think of all these years, when I have been sure you were one and the same man!"

RAM SINGH was waiting in the Daimler below, and the snow was sifting down softly in large, feathery flakes. He stood rigidly beside the doorway.

"It came over the air perfectly, Ram Singh," Wentworth said quietly, "have you already cleared the soundtrack of the speech?"

Ram Singh salaamed, *"Han, sahib!"* he growled, "but this Spider said some defaming things, master. When I get my hands upon his throat… Ha!" Ram Singh threw back his head and roared out his laughter on the cold night air.

Jackson shouldered forward, "Pipe down, you heathen," he rasped, in top-sergeant style. "You want to give the show away?"

Ram Singh cut his laughter short and scowled down at Jackson. "I will have thy ears yet, for my necklace, fool!"

Jackson snorted, "Only a weak sister like you would wear a necklace, and…."

Wentworth laughed, knowing that this was the reaction from the tension of long battle. Nita's hand was light on his arm, and the night seemed suddenly kind. The drifting snow-flakes were like a benison.

"Jackson," he said curtly. "You disobeyed orders!"

Jackson stiffened, and his face went suddenly rigid and pale. He faced Wentworth, standing at attention.

"Begging your pardon, Major," he said stiffly. "Regulations say, "When a superior officer is mentally or physically disqualified, it shall be the duty of the next ranking officer to take command, and to carry on to the best of his ability, disregarding any previous instructions if they shall interfere with what his knowledge dictates…!'"

Wentworth said, dryly, "That's a bit free in quotation, Jackson, but close enough. Jackson, you're confined to quarters for thirty days… and there will be bonus of a thousand dollars for you when you come out!"

Jackson saluted, and the laughter sparkled in his eyes. "Thank you, Major!" he said. His hand slapped against his thigh.

Ram Singh's teeth flashed whitely behind his beard. "Ah, hoo!" he chuckled. "And I shall be his jailer! Thou small flea…."

"You heathen lummox…."

Nita said softly, "You two brave splendid men!"

Jackson's ears turned red, and Ram Singh stiffened with pride… But Wentworth laughed and swept Nita into his arms, and climbed into the car.

"You splendid warriors are going to get your faces washed

with snow," he said dryly, "if we don't get home inside of five minutes. In fact, I shall call in the Spider to perform the task!"

They were all laughing, as the car rolled northward along Park, swung westward toward home… At his window high up in the apartment building, Kirkpatrick watched them go, and shook his head wonderingly over Cassidy. Standing straight up, with his shoulders hitched against the wall, Cassidy was asleep, a faithful guard worn out by the too hard performance of his duty.

He would sleep for twelve hours as Wentworth had ordered him, under the spell of hypnosis, but he would never remember opening the door of that cell for Wentworth to leave; or locking him in again when he returned.

Kirkpatrick smiled, "And all these years," he said to himself slowly, "I have suspected Dick of being the Spider! What a fool I have been. What a fool!"

❏ #4: The Suicide Squad in Corpse-Town — $14.95
❏ #5: Wanted–In Three Pine Coffins — $14.95
❏ #6: The Suicide Squad's Dawn Patrol — $14.95
❏ #7: Targets for the Flaming Arrow — $16.95

OPERATOR 5

❏ #1: The Masked Invasion — $13.95
❏ #2: The Invisible Empire — $13.95
❏ #3: The Yellow Scourge — $13.95
❏ #4: The Melting Death — $13.95
❏ #5: Cavern of the Damned — $13.95
❏ #6: Master of Broken Men — $13.95
❏ #7: Invasion of the Dark Legions — $13.95
❏ #8: The Green Death Mists — $13.95
❏ #9: Legions of Starvation — $13.95
❏ #10: The Red Invader — $13.95
❏ #11: The League of War-Monsters — $13.95
❏ #12: The Army of the Dead — $13.95
❏ #13: March of the Flame Marauders — $13.95
❏ #14: Blood Reign of the Dictator — $13.95
❏ #15: Invasion of the Yellow Warlords — $13.95
❏ #16: Legions of the Death Master — $13.95
❏ #17: Hosts of the Flaming Death — $13.95
❏ #18: Invasion of the Crimson Death Cult — $13.95
❏ #19: Attack of the Blizzard Men — $13.95
❏ #20: Scourge of the Invisible Death — $13.95
❏ #21: Raiders of the Red Death — $13.95
❏ #22: War-Dogs of the Green Destroyer — $13.95
❏ #23: Rockets From Hell — $13.95
❏ #24: War-Masters from the Orient — $13.95
❏ #25: Crime's Reign of Terror — $13.95
❏ #26: Death's Ragged Army — $13.95
❏ #27: Patriots' Death Battalion — $13.95
❏ #28: The Bloody Forty-five Days — $13.95
❏ #29: America's Plague Battalions — $13.95
❏ #30: Liberty's Suicide Legions — $13.95
❏ #31: Siege of the Thousand Patriots — $13.95
❏ #32: Patriots' Death March — $14.95
❏ #33: Revolt of the Lost Legions — $14.95
❏ #34: Drums of Destruction — $14.95
❏ #35: The Army Without a Country — $14.95
❏ #36: The Bloody Frontiers — $14.95
❏ #37: The Coming of the Mongol Hordes — $14.95
❏ #38: The Siege That Brought Black Death — $16.95
❏ #39: Revolt of the Devil Men — $16.95
❏ #40: The Suicide Battalion — $16.95
❏ **NEW**: #41: The Day of the Damned — $16.95

RED FINGER

❏ #1: Second-Hand Death — $24.95

G-8 AND HIS BATTLE ACES

❏ #1: The Bat Staffel — $13.95

CAPTAIN COMBAT

❏ #1: The Sky Beast of Berlin — $13.95
❏ #2: Red Wings For the Blood Battalion — $13.95
❏ #3: Low Ceiling For Nazi Hell Hawks — $13.95

DUSTY AYRES AND HIS BATTLE BIRDS

❏ #1: Black Lightning! — $13.95
❏ #2: Crimson Doom — $13.95
❏ #3: The Purple Tornado — $13.95
❏ #4: The Screaming Eye — $13.95
❏ #5: The Green Thunderbolt — $13.95
❏ #6: The Red Destroyer — $13.95
❏ #7: The White Death — $13.95
❏ #8: The Black Avenger — $13.95
❏ #9: The Silver Typhoon — $13.95
❏ #10: The Troposphere F-S — $13.95
❏ #11: The Blue Cyclone — $13.95
❏ #12: The Tesla Raiders — $13.95

MAVERICKS

❏ #1: Five Against the Law — $12.95
❏ #2: Mesquite Manhunters — $12.95
❏ #3: Bait for the Lobo Pack — $12.95
❏ #4: Doc Grimson's Outlaw Posse — $12.95
❏ #5: Charlie Parr's Gunsmoke Cure — $12.95

THE MYSTERIOUS WU FANG

❏ #1: The Case of the Six Coffins — $12.95
❏ #2: The Case of the Scarlet Feather — $12.95
❏ #3: The Case of the Yellow Mask — $12.95
❏ #4: The Case of the Suicide Tomb — $12.95
❏ #5: The Case of the Green Death — $12.95
❏ #6: The Case of the Black Lotus — $12.95
❏ #7: The Case of the Hidden Scourge — $12.95

THE SECRET 6

❏ #1: The Red Shadow — $13.95
❏ #2: House of Walking Corpses — $13.95
❏ #3: The Monster Murders — $13.95
❏ #4: The Golden Alligator — $13.95

CAPTAIN ZERO

❏ #1: City of Deadly Sleep — $13.95
❏ #2: The Mark of Zero! — $13.95
❏ #3: The Golden Murder Syndicate — $13.95